NOBODY'S THERE

ALSO AVAILABLE IN LAUREL-LEAF BOOKS:

NOBODY'S THERE

JOAN LOWERY NIXON

Published by
Dell Laurel-Leaf
an imprint of
Random House Children's Books
a division of Random House, Inc.
1540 Broadway
New York, New York 10036

Visit us on the Web! www.randomhouse.com/teens

Educators and librarians, for a variety of teaching tools, visit us at
www.randomhouse.com/teachers

ISBN: 0-440-22760-7

RL: 5.3

Reprinted by arrangement with Delacorte Press

Printed in the United States of America

November 2001

10 9 8 7 6 5 4 3 2 1

OPM

NOBODY'S THERE

CHAPTER ONE

Trembling, her legs so wobbly it was hard to stand, Abbie Thompson clung to the rough trunk of an oak tree and waited for her father to appear. As a garish yellow porch light over the nearest apartment suddenly gleamed, Abbie sucked in her breath and slid farther back into the darkness behind the wide tree trunk.

Abbie knew she shouldn't be here. She shouldn't be spying. She'd die if her father saw her. Fearing to be seen, she had pulled a scarf over her strawberry-blond hair, which was light enough to stand out in the darkness. She must not be caught lurking, but she had to know. She had to!

The door of the apartment opened, and Davis

Thompson stepped out, hand in hand with a young, very pretty, dark-haired woman. Both of them tall, trim, and attractive, they moved as though they knew they were an exceptionally good-looking pair. Laughing, they drew close to each other, and he bent to kiss her.

It was a light, quick kiss, but Abbie doubled over in pain. It felt as if someone had socked her hard in the stomach.

She watched her father and the woman run to his low-slung red sports car. Before she could react, before she could think, the car had driven away.

Abbie let herself slide to the ground, sitting cross-legged in the dark. She stared at the still-bright front window of the apartment, hating the woman who lived there and hating her father.

All through the seventeen years of her life, Davis Thompson had called Abbie "Daddy's girl," and she had loved this special nickname. He had been a real daddy then. He'd played ball with her and gone to her Fathers' Night dinners at school and applauded her piano playing at recitals. Lately, though, he had become so different that Abbie wondered if he could possibly be the same person.

Davis Thompson—known to nearly everyone in the south Gulf Coast town of Buckler, Texas, as Dr. Davis Thompson, professor of English at Buckler College—suddenly dyed his hair to cover the gray at his temples, wore expensive sports coats over cashmere turtleneck sweaters, bought a car that would fit a movie star's lifestyle, and walked out on his family.

"You must understand, Sandra, I'm not being fulfilled any longer," her father had told Abbie's mother just before he left. "Life should be rich and complete."

"Davis, are you serious?" Mrs. Thompson's voice had wavered with shock.

He raised his voice as if he were arguing not only with her, but with himself. "I've given this sincere and weighty consideration," he said. "For a long time I've felt that my life here is nothing."

Frozen in the hallway, Abbie couldn't help overhearing the conversation. She had gasped and leaned against the wall for support. Mom and Davy and she were *nothing*?

"Is there someone else?" Abbie's mother had asked. Her voice came out raspy and choked, and she had to ask the question again.

"Be reasonable," Dr. Thompson had said. "It wasn't working with us. You know that."

"No, I didn't know. I thought . . . well . . . your moodiness . . . I mean, when you didn't get the promotion to department head, I assumed . . ."

"Perhaps I would have got it, if I'd had more support from you," Dr. Thompson had snapped.

"More support?" Mrs. Thompson's voice had risen. "After all I've done—"

But the back door had slammed shut. Realizing that her father had left, Abbie had run to cling to her mom.

Now Abbie dug her fingers into the circle of freshly turned earth that surrounded the tree. As her hands slid over the ring of small, smooth stones that bordered the circle, she whispered to her absent father over and over, "How could you not want us? How could you?"

She tried to look away from the lighted apartment window. Behind the golden glow lived the woman with the dark hair, the woman who had kissed her father.

The pain in Abbie's mind and body turned to an anger hot and intense. Breathing heavily, she unconsciously gripped the stones, pulling them from their ring as she rose to her feet. She stepped out from under the wide limbs of the oak, aimed at the window, and threw the stones as hard as she could.

"I hate you! I hate you!" she yelled.

The glass smashed, gold-red splinters flying to each side like starbursts. There was a moment of total silence, as though the air had stopped moving. Then a young woman in a robe, her blond hair wet and stringy, ran screaming from the apartment. Doors of other apartments opened, and people scurried out, scrambling without direction like ants whose hill has been disturbed. A beefy man in his undershirt grabbed Abbie's arms. A plump woman kept yelling that she had called the police.

Abbie stood numbly, the red anger draining from her mind and body, as she tried to remember what she had done.

Like an automaton Abbie moved through the

4

next few hours. She was driven in a police car to the station, where someone asked her a million questions, then fingerprinted and photographed her.

Her mother appeared, tear streaks on her face. "Oh, Abbie! Oh, darling, I'll help you. This is all your stupid, stupid father's fault."

Dr. Thompson arrived, scowling. "What a foolish thing to do, Abbie! What could you have been thinking? You can thank me for talking Jamie and her roommate out of pressing charges."

But local officials had recently waged war on malicious mischief. Getting tough on these troublemaking kids was a priority, and Abbie found herself sitting in an office opposite a man who introduced himself as Judge Arnold Wilhite.

The judge reminded Abbie of her late grandfather Bill, with his thin hair combed over his bald spot, and crinkle lines around his eyes. Judge Wilhite leaned back in his office chair and rested his tooled cowboy boots on his desk. "I want to hear what *you* have to say, Abigail. Why'd you throw rocks through Miss—" He stopped and glanced at the paper on his desk. "—through the window of Miss Jamie Lane's apartment?"

So that was her name—Jamie Lane, Abbie thought. "I guess I don't have a good reason," she told the judge. She stared at her hands, which were clenched in her lap. "I just did it." The numbness she had felt began to slide away, and Abbie was frightened. She breathed in small, shallow gasps, trying to steady herself.

Judge Wilhite studied Abbie for a few minutes.

Then he said, "The D.A.'s office is talking about prosecuting you for malicious mischief. Is that what you'd call what you did? Malicious mischief?"

Abbie raised her head and looked at him. "It wasn't mischief. It was hate. I hated her, and I was angry."

"Had you given this act some thought? Had you planned to come to Miss Lane's apartment and throw rocks?"

"No. I didn't even think about it while I was throwing the rocks. It's just that when my father kissed her . . ." Abbie stopped speaking and looked down at her hands again, surprised that her fingers looked like twisted spiders' legs and her knuckles stood out like small white knobs.

"Do you regret what you've done?"

"No! I mean, I'm sorry I scared that woman's roommate. I didn't know she had a roommate. But I'm not going to apologize to my father or to . . . that woman."

"Although you're a first-time offender, the response to teenagers' breaking the law is getting tougher and tougher." The judge thought a moment, then asked, "Abbie, have you ever heard of deferred adjudication?"

She shook her head, and he answered, "*Adjudication* means my decision. *Deferred* means I can put off giving my decision."

"I don't understand," Abbie replied. "Why should you put off making a decision?"

"Because of what might take place in the meantime." With a thump Judge Wilhite's boots landed on the floor, and he leaned forward, elbows on his desk. "You're seventeen. Do you have a Texas driver's license?"

"Yes," Abbie said.

"Is there an automobile at your disposal?"

Abbie shrugged. "Mom has let me drive her car when I have to stay late at school for something and can't take the school bus. When that happens she takes the city bus to the office where she works. She's in the finance department for a real estate company and—"

The judge waved his hand, and Abbie stopped in midsentence. "Do you have an after-school job?" he asked.

"No."

"Extracurricular activities that keep you busy?"

"Not very busy. I'm in the choral group, and I thought about maybe signing up for yearbook staff." Abbie shivered. She didn't know what the judge was trying to find out. Was she giving the wrong answers?

"Do you keep up your grades?"

Abbie ached as she stared into the judge's dark and penetrating eyes. He could read her mind. She was sure he could. So why was he asking so many questions? She took a deep breath and answered, "My grades have always been good—until lately. Lately, I haven't wanted to study. I haven't cared."

Do you know what it's like to be considered a nothing—a nobody? she thought. *Why should a nothing care about studying or grades or anything else?*

7

Judge Wilhite bent over his desk, writing something. Abbie waited. Then he said, "I'm going to put you on probation for one year, Abigail. I'm going to give you a job to do, and you're going to show me that you can do it well. At the end of the year, under the decree of deferred adjudication, all record of your arrest will be wiped out. You'll have a clean slate. Got it?"

Abbie knew he was waiting for her to thank him. But she didn't care if she had a clean slate. She didn't care that he seemed to be doing her a huge favor. "What kind of a job?" she asked.

"The Buckler Women's Club has recently set up a program to aid elderly women in the community," he said. "It's called Friend to Friend. Teenage volunteers are matched with older women who live alone. Each morning, at a set time, the girls telephone the women to make sure they're okay. Most of these women can no longer drive and they have no family member at hand to drive for them, so the girls take on this job. Two or three days a week after school or on weekends they drive the women to the grocery store, or sometimes to a department store, or to the senior citizens' center. Often, with their families, they take the women to church on Sundays.

"I think highly of this program," Judge Wilhite added, "perhaps because my wife is president of Friend to Friend, and she tells me about the success stories they've had."

Abbie stared at him. "You want me to take care of some old lady?"

"Not 'some old lady.' One particular elderly

8

woman who needs assistance. You'll soon know her by name and become acquainted with her."

"I haven't got time," Abbie protested.

"Sure you have."

Tears blurred Abbie's vision. With the back of one hand she wiped them away. "I know what you're doing," she blurted out. "You're trying to keep me so busy I can't get into more trouble. For your information, I'm not going to throw rocks. I'm not going near that . . . that woman. I'm never going to see her or my father again."

"That's up to you," the judge said quietly. "I had hoped you'd understand what I'm trying to do for you. I'm not going to explain it to you. I'll let you figure it out yourself."

As he stood and walked toward the door, Abbie realized he wanted her to leave. She stumbled to her feet and followed him.

"By noon tomorrow, you'll receive the name of the woman with whom you'll be paired. I want you to call on her. Visit her house, as soon as you've read the material in the packet. Got it?"

"Got it," Abbie mumbled.

"Look at me, Abigail."

Abbie raised her head and did as he had asked. She wished Judge Wilhite didn't look so much like her grandfather. Her grandfather had been kind and full of laughter and fun. He wouldn't have punished her by giving her a horrible job like this. But the judge had laugh lines around the corners of his mouth and eyes too. Maybe he liked to laugh. Maybe he had grandchildren. Tears burned her eyes again.

"I'm going to talk to your mother and father and to the attorneys out there. Please wait here with my secretary. It won't be long before you and your mother will be free to leave and go home," the judge said.

Abbie nodded. The words escaped before she could stop them. "Thank you," she said.

Judge Wilhite smiled, and all the crinkle lines deepened. "Wait until one year from now," he said. "Then I think you'll really mean it."

CHAPTER TWO

Later, as Abbie and her mother drove home, the sea air damp against their skin, they both cried a little.

"I guess I've been too concerned with my own problems. But I just can't believe that your father would—" Mrs. Thompson broke off, took a long breath, and said, "It has to be my fault. I've let you down."

"No, you haven't, Mom. It's not your fault. It's Dad's. I hate him for leaving us, for not wanting us."

Mrs. Thompson whirled to stare in surprise at Abbie. "Not wanting you?"

"Watch it, Mom! The light's changing."

The car rocked as Mrs. Thompson slammed

her foot on the brake. "Listen to me, Abbie," she said. "Your father wasn't leaving you and Davy. He loves you both."

"No, he doesn't."

"Yes, he does," she answered, "as much as he can love anybody besides himself."

Abbie sighed. "I don't want to talk about Dad, Mom. I can't take it. I don't want to talk about *anything*."

Mrs. Thompson reached over and patted Abbie's arm. "All right, sweetheart. I understand." She mumbled something under her breath, then glanced at the brightly lit numbers on the car's clock. "At least we'll be home before ten. Mrs. Erwin's staying with Davy, and she lets him stay up later than he should."

As they turned into their driveway, Abbie broke her silence. "Mom," she said, "do I have to do what the judge told me? I mean about babysitting some old—uh—elderly woman?"

"I'm afraid so, Abbie," her mother answered. "Your father said he couldn't afford to help in getting you a secondhand car, which doesn't surprise me. Just look at the expensive sports car *he's* driving! So for a year you'll use my car on certain days after school and on Saturdays, and I'll catch the bus. That should make him happy. Well, never mind that he's no help and doesn't care. *I* care. I'm not going to let you be prosecuted for . . ."

Her voice broke, and it took a few moments before she could continue. She put on a light smile and the same aren't-we-going-to-love-this tone she used with Davy every time she came up with some new healthful casserole. "The judge explained the Friend to Friend program, and it sounds okay. According to him, many of the girls and the women they're assigned to have become close friends."

Close friends? Abbie hated the idea. She already had close friends. She didn't need new friends—especially women older than her own grandmothers.

But in the morning Judge Wilhite's wife telephoned early. Abbie was munching through a bowl of cereal and staring blankly at the row of small, colorful cream pitchers that marched across the kitchen windowsill, when the phone rang and she reached for it. "Hello," she said. Overbright sunlight blasted through the window, ricocheting off the polished wooden table, and the blare of Davy's Saturday-morning cartoons made her head ache.

"I'm sorry," Abbie continued. She motioned to Davy to turn down the sound of the television. "I didn't hear you. Who did you say you were?"

The woman's voice was steely. "Why don't you turn off those cartoons, please?"

Abbie grabbed the remote control out of Davy's hand and turned off the television. "I'm sorry," she said again. "My little brother—"

"Please pay attention," the woman said. "As I told you, my name is Judith Wilhite. I'm president of the organization Friend to Friend."

"Oh—oh, y-yes," Abbie stammered. She sat on the remote control and turned her back so that she didn't have to look at the faces Davy was making at her. "I'm Abbie—uh—Abigail Th—"

"I know. My husband informed me about you and your circumstances." Mrs. Wilhite's words remained so clipped and cold that Abbie hunched her shoulders, her back pressing uncomfortably against her kitchen chair.

"The girls who are volunteers in our program are top students and leaders in their high schools. It's certainly not standard rules or even good judgment to add to this outstanding group a girl who has been in criminal trouble and is on probation. However, my husband has convinced me to give you a try."

Sick at heart, Abbie struggled to keep her mind on what Mrs. Wilhite was saying. Criminal trouble? A girl on probation? The label made Abbie feel like some terrible kind of lowlife.

"Gimme!" Davy said, and held out his hand for the remote control.

Mrs. Wilhite told Abbie that a package of information had been sent by messenger to her home. "Please read all the rules carefully. If there are any questions, just telephone our secretary's number on the first sheet of the booklet. I believe you agreed to pay an afternoon call today on the woman who'll be assigned to you?"

"Yes, ma'am," Abbie answered.

"Very well," Mrs. Wilhite said. "I hope there won't be any problems."

"No, there won't," Abbie said, but Mrs. Wilhite had already hung up the phone.

"Before Mom went to her office, she said I could watch Saturday-morning cartoons!" Davy yelled at Abbie. "Gimme back the control."

Abbie sighed and handed Davy the remote control. He didn't used to be so argumentative. He'd always been a happy kid, and they'd had fun together. Now he was angry most of the time. He hadn't heard Dad's parting words, as Abbie had, but it didn't matter. Davy must still feel as rejected as Abbie did.

"That was an important phone call," she tried to explain. "It was all about something I have to do to make up for what happened last night."

Davy clutched the remote control, but he didn't turn on the television. He cocked his head, studying Abbie with curiosity. "You threw rocks at Dad and his girlfriend," he said. "I heard some of what Mom said to Mrs. Erwin."

"I didn't throw rocks at anybody," Abbie told him. "Dad and . . . that woman had already driven off. I threw them at the front window of her apartment. I didn't know she had a room-mate and she'd be there."

Davy smiled. "I wish I'd seen that. I wish I'd seen the police come. Did they have their sirens on?"

Abbie groaned. "I shouldn't have done it, Davy. I was angry. I wasn't thinking. No matter how I felt about what Dad was doing, I shouldn't have thrown the rocks. Do you understand that what I did was wrong, and now I have to make up for it?"

"They didn't put you in jail."

"No, but I'm on probation. The judge gave me a job to do. That's what the phone call was all about. Do you want me to tell you more?"

"No," Davy said. He held out the remote control toward the television set and turned his back on Abbie.

Before the package arrived, Abbie put the dishes in the dishwasher, changed the sheets on the beds, added some towels to the laundry, and put the first load into the washer. Then just as ordered, she sat down and read everything in the large envelope. The printed flyers and letter told her the same things the judge had said, but they also gave her a name, phone number, and address.

The telephone rang again, and Abbie grabbed it before Davy could get to it.

A familiar voice said, "Hi, Abbie. Want to go to the mall this afternoon?"

Abbie leaned into the warmth of Gigi's best-friendship, pulling it around her shoulders, clinging to its support. "I can't," she answered. "Today I have to visit the woman I was assigned to."

Abbie explained about the Friend to Friend program. "Mrs. Wilhite made it clear I wouldn't fit in with the other girls in the program. They're all straight-A students, at the tops of their classes." She smiled as she added, "Like you."

"I know about the program," Gigi said. "Wendy Banes is in it. So is Judy Hanks." Then she added, "Tell me, what is your assignment like? How old is she? Do you have to spoon-feed her or anything like that?"

Abbie laughed. Gigi always had a way of making her feel better, no matter what the problem. Gigi had immediately understood how Abbie felt about her father; and the night before, when Abbie had told Gigi about why she'd been arrested, Gigi had insisted that she not blame herself, that anyone would have done the exact same thing.

"I can't answer your questions, because I haven't met the woman yet," Abbie said.

"Do you know her name?"

"Edna Merkel, 6615 Darnell Street," Abbie read aloud, and sighed. "I have no idea what she's like."

"I know," Gigi said. "I can picture her in my mind. She's way overweight, with thin white hair and thick ankles, and she's probably at least a hundred years old. She nibbles on chocolates and giggles when she talks and wears some kind of sweet perfume that smells like marshmallows."

Abbie laughed again. "Right. And her dresses are printed cotton housedresses, which she saved from the forties."

"And tidy little hats."

"With veils and one red rose."

"No. One yellow sunflower."

Abbie and Gigi both broke into laughter. As soon as they calmed down, Gigi said, "Call me when you get back from visiting her and tell me everything. Okay?"

"Will do," Abbie said. "I gotta go now. I'll talk to you later."

As she hung up the telephone, Abbie's good mood vanished. She would soon meet Edna Merkel, and for better or worse she was stuck with her.

"I can't take it," Abbie murmured, but as soon as her Saturday-morning chores were finished and her mother had returned from her half-day at work, Abbie borrowed the car and drove to Edna Merkel's house on Darnell.

It was a small two-story brick building on a street of similar houses, built so near the gulf that the air carried a clinging fragrance of salt and seaweed. Abbie guessed that the houses in Mrs. Merkel's neighborhood had all been built at the same time, probably way back in the thirties, or even the twenties.

Six steps led up to a deep, covered front porch that extended across the front of Edna Merkel's house. Although the day was flooded with sunshine, thick vines of Confederate jasmine twined up the pillars and dripped over the roof, creating a dim, cool cavern.

Abbie pushed the doorbell and heard it chime off key, but no one came to the door. Impatiently Abbie jabbed the doorbell again.

Suddenly the dark-stained front door slowly opened an inch. "Get off my porch," a voice rasped.

Startled, Abbie jumped back. Then she remembered why she had come and knew that she had to be there. She peered into the darkness behind the open crack in the door but couldn't see a face she could talk to. "Mrs. Merkel, I'm Abbie Thompson," she said. "I was sent here by the president of Friend to Friend."

18

"I'm going to count to three," the voice said.

"I'm supposed to telephone you and visit you and drive you to places you want to go and—"

"And then I shoot. One . . . two . . ."

Abbie whirled and ran down the steps of the porch.

CHAPTER THREE

----

anting with fear, Abbie raced as far as the sidewalk.

"Wait a minute!" Mrs. Merkel shouted in a voice so strident and raspy that Abbie winced. "Did you say you'd drive me where I want to go? Like at two o'clock today?"

Abbie turned back, shakily retracing a few steps toward the house.

"Well? Speak up."

Framed in the open doorway stood a tall, bony woman with gray hair pulled tightly away from her face and tied at the nape of her neck with a string. She was dressed in an odd combination of an oversized, faded green T-shirt advertising a celebrity golf classic and a lined, flowered chiffon skirt that hung almost to her ankles. Navy blue ankle socks and smudged white tennies completed her outfit. As she waited for an answer, her heavy-lidded, dark eyes cut into Abbie like a pair of lasers. For a moment Abbie could only stare.

"Stop gawking. I'm not trying to make the cover of *Vogue*," Mrs. Merkel said. "And come back here. We can't just yell at each other."

Abbie took a few more steps, then stopped. "I don't want you to shoot me," she said.

Mrs. Merkel shrugged. "Don't be so quick to believe everything people tell you. I don't own a gun. I just don't like to be bothered by people I don't know, so I scare them away." Her eyes drilled even deeper. "Come on up here on the porch. You said you'd take me anywhere I wanted to go. Did you mean it, or was that just so much blather?"

Abbie forced herself to walk to the porch. "I meant it," she said. She tried to keep the bitterness from her voice as she added, "The judge said I had to."

"You *had* to? Well, aren't you a polite, gracious little thing?" Mrs. Merkel stepped closer and looked Abbie up and down. "Not so little, I guess. I'm five feet eight, and you're every inch as tall as I am."

Abbie could feel herself blushing with embarrassment, and she hated it. She hated this horrible old woman, and she hated the judge and his wife. She took a deep breath to steady herself, then said, "I'm sorry. I meant that I was assigned to the Friend to Friend program." Without flinching, she looked Mrs. Merkel in the eye. "I threw rocks through the window of a woman's apartment. I was caught and given this assignment as a condition of probation. That's the story."

"I know the story. I know just about everything that goes on around here." She shook her head. "So they sent you to me, did they?"

Abbie was startled when Mrs. Merkel bent over, making a strange, cackling noise in her throat. Was she choking? As she moved closer she saw that Mrs. Merkel was laughing.

"I get a lawbreaker and you get me. Fair enough trade," she said. She motioned toward a wooden porch swing, its varnish weathered in decayed blotches. "Don't just stand there like a ninny. Sit down."

Abbie sat gingerly, concerned that the rusty chains that held the old swing in place might give, dropping her to the floor.

But Mrs. Merkel plopped down beside her, saying, "It's not going to fall apart. Last time my nephew Charlie drove down from Dallas, he checked the bolts and made sure they'd hold." Pushing off with her oversized tennis shoes, she set the swing gently in motion.

"That Friend to Friend baloney is a bunch of garbage," she said. "The first two girls they sent me didn't have half a brain between them, no matter that I was told they were honor students." She studied Abbie. "Threw rocks at your dad's girlfriend, did you? Hmmm. Is that what honor students are doing lately?"

"I didn't throw rocks at her. I threw them at her apartment," Abbie answered.

Mrs. Merkel grinned. "Fat lot of good it did you. I hope you figured out by this time that wasn't very bright. Now, stop dithering around and get back to what we were talking about. Are you or are you not going to drive me wherever I want to go this afternoon?"

"I said I would." Abbie spaced her words slowly, trying to hold her temper.

"I suppose you'd like to drive to Mexico," Mrs. Merkel said. "A lot of criminals take off and run down there and hope they won't get extradited back to the U.S., where they'd have to stand trial. That should be just the place for you."

Indignantly Abbie gripped the arm of the swing. "I don't run away from my problems," she said.

"You can't take a joke so good either," Mrs. Merkel snapped. She looked at her watch. "You got any idea where the community center is? Probably not. Kids of today are so wrapped up in their own snotty little worlds, they don't think about anybody or anything else."

"I know where the center is," Abbie answered. It was getting more and more difficult to talk to this crabby old woman without exploding at her.

Mrs. Merkel suddenly stood, rocking the swing and throwing Abbie off balance. "Then come on," she said. "What are you waiting for?"

As she followed Mrs. Merkel toward the Thompsons' car, Abbie's anger shot like burning arrows toward Judge Wilhite's judgmental wife. She hated her.

You set me up, Abbie accused the woman who had scorned her over the phone. *You knew what Mrs. Merkel was like. You knew she had kicked out two girls before I came along. She'd kick me out too. You were sure she would. And then you could prove to your husband that he'd been wrong and you'd been right.*

Abbie opened the passenger door for Mrs. Merkel, trying hard not to slam it as Mrs. Merkel settled herself on the seat with the comment, "I don't expect you to be a good driver. Kids today are reckless hooligans on the road."

For only a few seconds Abbie wearily leaned against the car, again directing her thoughts to a smirking Mrs. Wilhite. *You just think you're going to win this one. You're not. I'm not going to give up this easily. I'll stick it out with Mrs. Merkel, no matter what, and win that deferred adjudication I was promised. Just wait and see.*

At the blast of the car's horn, Abbie jumped back with a yelp. She hurried around to the driver's side, climbed in, and fastened her seat belt. Glancing at Mrs. Merkel, she said, "Please fasten your seat belt."

"I don't like seat belts."

"There's a two-hundred-dollar fine if you don't wear your seat belt," Abbie persisted. "It's the law."

Mrs. Merkel grinned. "You're a fine one to be quoting the law. Tell me about the law against throwing rocks."

Abbie took a deep breath. *What do I do with this woman? Do I just give up and tell Mrs. Wilhite, "You win"?* Abbie looked into Mrs. Merkel's eyes and shivered at the malice she saw there. *No,* she thought. *I won't give up.*

Finally Mrs. Merkel snapped the seat belt in place and grumbled, "You were certainly taking your own sweet time out there. What's the point of going to the meeting of my book club if I can't get there when it starts?"

Abbie looked at the clock on the dashboard as she started the car and pulled into the street. "It's barely twenty minutes to two," she said. "You told me your meeting begins at two, and we're only ten minutes away from the community center on Waterfront Drive."

"Ten minutes if you speed—which you probably will."

"Tell me about your book club," Abbie said. She turned onto Main Street and drove a short two blocks toward Waterfront Drive, where she turned again, heading south.

Golden shimmers of sunlight rippled over the water, and out in the bay at least two dozen sailboats skimmed the waves. March was always a beautiful month, and this day seemed one of its best.

"Watch out for that truck. Over there at the corner."

"I see the truck."

"There's a man down there going to cross the street."

"I see him."

Mrs. Merkel took her eyes from the road long enough to examine the interior of the car. She ran her long, bony fingers over the upholstery. "This isn't much of a car," she said. "But then, it doesn't make much sense to spend good money on a car for a kid, who's only going to smash it up anyway."

"It's not my car," Abbie told her. "It belongs to my mother." Abbie realized that Mrs. Merkel was studying her from the corner of her eye, but she refused to look at the woman. "Tell me about some of your friends in the book club," she said.

"Friends? Huh! I wouldn't call them friends." Mrs. Merkel's voice was bitter. "Lawanda and Gladys used to pick me up for meetings, but they haven't for a long time now. Always one dumb excuse after another, until I stopped calling them. Huh!" she said again. "Who needs them?"

With Mrs. Merkel's nonstop directions, Abbie turned into the parking lot of the community center and pulled up to the front door. "You can get out here. I'll park the car and meet you inside," she said.

Mrs. Merkel's eyes narrowed. "Maybe I should stick with you—like a parole officer, or whoever you have to report to. Make sure you don't run off and leave me while you got the chance."

Abbie sighed, Mrs. Wilhite's smirk in her

mind. "Trust me," she said. "I'm not going anywhere."

"I don't trust anybody," Mrs. Merkel snapped, but she climbed out of the car and slammed the door.

To Abbie's surprise, Mrs. Merkel waited for her at the door so that they could walk into the center together. With Mrs. Merkel leading, they made their way into one of the smaller meeting rooms, where a cluster of six senior citizens were informally chatting.

A hefty woman, her tight curls more gray than black, was saying, "So when she finally came to she saw right away he was dead!"

No one responded. They all turned toward the doorway staring at Mrs. Merkel.

A short, plump woman with thin white hair clasped her hands together and smiled nervously. "Oh, Edna dear, it's you," she said.

"As usual, you're right on top of things, aren't you, Gladys?" Edna's voice was thick with sarcasm. She strode across the room to join the group. "I would have come to some of the other book club meetings if anybody had given me a ride."

A wave of guilt splashed over Gladys's face. "Oh, dear," she murmured. With a visible effort she recovered and added, "We're glad you're back, dear."

"Not all of us," one of the men growled. Although he spoke to himself, his words were loud enough to be heard.

"I didn't expect you to cheer, Jose," Mrs. Merkel said, "since I'm the only one around here with enough smarts and gumption to disagree with your lame opinions."

Jose muttered something under his breath, but Gladys smiled at Abbie and asked, "Who is this dear girl? Is this a granddaughter we didn't know about?"

Abbie braced herself for whatever Mrs. Merkel might blurt out about her arrest and probation. *I don't know these people*, she thought. *What difference does it make what they think about me?*

She was surprised when Mrs. Merkel smugly announced, "This is Abbie Thompson. She's my driver."

"Oooh! You have a driver. How lovely," the short woman said. She put an arm around Abbie and patted her shoulder. "I'm Gladys Partridge, and it's so nice to have you here, dear."

"Don't get too chummy," Mrs. Merkel said. "Abbie's on probation. If you're smart, you'll keep a wary eye on her."

Abbie flinched as Gladys stepped back and one of the other women whispered, "Is she a gang member?"

With a smile Jose took Abbie's arm. "If you're going to be a regular I'll introduce you. We'll start with me. I'm Jose Morales."

Although Mrs. Merkel scowled her disapproval, Jose made the circle, introducing Abbie first to the woman whose story they'd interrupted, Lawanda Truitt. The others were Olivia Barton, Dolores Garcia, and Sam Granby. Abbie was grateful for Jose's kindness and tried her hardest to remember their names, settling on first names only. Gladys was short and sweet; Lawanda was tall and heavy; Dolores was round and smiley; Olivia was small and quiet; Jose was leather-skinned and bushy-browed; and Sam was tall, bony, and easygoing.

Lawanda leaned toward Mrs. Merkel. "Did you read the papers this morning? We were talkin' about the murder."

"Delmar Hastings, the bank president," Sam said.

"Gulf East Savings and Loan," Dolores added.

Olivia sighed and said, "His poor wife. At least his children were grown."

Lawanda took a step forward, picking up where she had left off. "I was sayin', when you came in, that Irene Conley—you know Irene. She's the head cashier in Gulf East Savings and Loan—Anyhow, Irene come to, after bein' hit on the head, and there was her boss lyin' on the floor, shot dead in a pool of blood."

Gladys closed her eyes. "Delmar Hastings, the bank president," she whispered.

"I know all that. I read the paper," Mrs. Merkel grumbled.

Abbie *hadn't* read the newspaper or listened to the morning TV news, so she paid close attention.

"Irene told the reporter from the *Buckler Bee* that she was hit on the head from behind, so she didn't even see who did it," Lawanda said.

"*Whodunnit*," Dolores corrected. "That's what they say on TV shows—*whodunnit*."

Lawanda continued. "I heard on the news this morning that Irene is in such a state she's confined to bed. Won't even talk to the TV or newspaper reporters."

"Why didn't the murderer kill Irene, too?" Mrs. Merkel asked.

Dolores shivered. "Edna, you sound so bloodthirsty."

Jose shook his head. "She's not bloodthirsty. She's not good at figuring things out. Anybody would know why it happened the way it did. Hastings saw the murderer's face and would have been able to identify him. Irene didn't and couldn't."

Mrs. Merkel snapped, "Since you're a lawbreaker, you'd know how the criminal mind works, if anybody would."

Jose's eyes flashed with anger. "You're the worst kind of backstabbing snitch. The world would be better off without you in it."

"Now, now," Gladys said, stepping between them. "That unpleasant business is over. Let's change the subject."

"Is it over? Not likely," Mrs. Merkel said. The look she gave Jose made Abbie think of blowguns and poison darts.

Dolores stepped between Jose and Mrs. Merkel. "Speaking of Irene," she said, "I heard Irene didn't even need that job. Mavis in the beauty parlor said that Irene's parents were the Buck Steavers. You've heard of the Buck Steavers."

"I haven't," Mrs. Merkel said.

"Oh. Well, most people have . . . I think.

30

Buck Steaver owned a lot of oil wells up in Beaumont. He was really, *really* rich, according to Mavis. Anyhow, he and his wife left Irene a lot of money."

Gladys nodded. "Then that's why Irene had such a nice car and pretty clothes," she said. She hesitated. "Unless it's her husband who's rich."

"Her husband sells appliances," Dolores answered. "You know—at that big appliance store out near the college. He's not about to make the fortune her parents did."

"Is he the bald man—the one who always wears bow ties?"

Mrs. Merkel snorted. "When are you two going to learn to stick to a subject? Are you talking about a murder in Buckler or about bow ties?"

Olivia spoke up shyly. "I don't understand how the murder could have happened. I keep reading in the *Bee* that the federal government has statistics to prove that the crime rate has gone down."

Sam's slow drawl emphasized his words. "It don't matter what the statistics say. All that counts is that a man got murdered in our own neighborhood."

"I use that bank," Gladys said.

"So do I." Lawanda nodded emphatically.

Mrs. Merkel frowned at everyone. "We all do. That's not news. And we don't know anything about the murder that wasn't in the paper, so let's get down to business. What's the book y'all have up for discussion today?"

Gladys smiled. "We aren't going to discuss books today, dear. We have a guest speaker."

31

Mrs. Merkel scowled. "We don't need a guest speaker. We're a book club. We're supposed to discuss books."

Gladys patted Mrs. Merkel's arm as she glanced toward the doorway. Her smile suddenly grew broader. "Sit down, dear," she said. "Here's our speaker now."

A young woman, dressed in a dark blue police officer's uniform and carrying a clipboard, strode briskly into the room.

Abbie started at the sight of the uniform, her heart thumping. "I'm here, like I'm supposed to be!" she wanted to shout. "Don't take me back to the judge!"

But the officer paid no special attention to Abbie. She shook hands with each of the book club members in turn, introducing herself as Amanda Martin.

When she held out a hand to Edna Merkel, it was ignored. Mrs. Merkel aimed her laser glance at Officer Martin and snapped at her, "What does a cop know about books?"

"Books?" The officer blinked.

"Yes, books. This is a book club. We talk about books. Or maybe you haven't figured that out yet. I guess with being so busy making the crime rate go down, cops need all the help they can get."

Gladys nervously waved her hands. "Edna, Officer Martin is our guest speaker. I told you we were going to have a guest speaker."

Mrs. Merkel shrugged, and her sarcasm deepened. "Don't guest speakers at book clubs speak about books?"

Officer Martin smiled. "Not this time," she said. "I asked Mrs. Partridge, as club president, for permission to speak to your group about a very important project we're starting in Buckler." She looked directly into Mrs. Merkel's eyes as she added, "You were right when you said cops need all the help we can get. We have to catch some mean, no-good crooks who are victimizing people in Buckler, and that's why I'm here—to ask for your help."

CHAPTER FOUR

Mrs. Merkel shoved between Gladys and Olivia in the front row of folding chairs. Abbie took a seat at the back.

Officer Martin began her speech. "During the past few years thieves and con artists have set their sights on senior citizens. Older people are vulnerable to this type of crime because they tend to be more trusting and less suspicious. There are many crooks right here in Buckler who need to be stopped. There are repair companies that promise to do work, collect their money, and disappear. Or people who advertise a specific product for sale, then substitute something else."

"They call that bait and switch." Gladys looked pleased with herself.

"Right. And people who telephone about something 'free' you've won, then tell you that you have to send money in order to get it."

"If anyone falls for that scam, he's stupid," Mrs. Merkel interrupted.

"No. Not stupid. Duped."

"Same thing."

Officer Martin went on. "Some scam artists try to get you to tell them your credit card number over the phone. Or they say they're collecting money for relief funds that don't exist. The list goes on and on, and it means that every day people right here in Buckler are losing a great deal of money to these crooks."

"What are we supposed to do about it?" Mrs. Merkel blurted out. "You want us to send sympathy cards?"

"Edna, dear," Gladys began.

But Jose snapped, "Shut your mouth up, Edna, and let the police officer say what she's got to say."

With all the book club members glaring at her, Mrs. Merkel leaned back in her chair, folded her arms across her chest, and scowled.

Officer Martin smiled and continued. "A few years ago the Houston Better Business Bureau founded an organization that called upon senior citizens to protect other senior citizens. They named it Silver Sleuths. They've had great success with it. We're setting up a similar organization in Buckler and calling it the Buckler Senior Citizens' Brigade. We've had an enthusiastic response from other seniors in

35

Buckler, and I hope your group will join us too."

Mrs. Merkel broke her short silence. "I don't like that name," she grumbled. "In the first place, I don't like to be called a senior citizen, as if I had to be reminded how old I am. And *Brigade* sounds like something from a 1940s army movie."

"Edna, I already told you to be quiet and listen for a change," Jose snapped. "You don't know everything, even if you think you do." He nodded toward Officer Martin. "Go ahead. Don't pay any attention to Edna."

Officer Martin hesitated only a moment. Then, with her eyes on Mrs. Merkel, she said, "Those of you who volunteer will be trained for various jobs. Some of you will help us in our office or answer our special phone line for senior citizens' questions or complaints about a company. Some of you will be our eyes and ears in the community. You'll check out ads, making sure consumers won't be tricked. You'll track down scams and fraudulent schemes."

"Humph! You make us sound like a pack of bloodhounds," Edna mumbled.

The officer continued. "We plan to set up a special hotline. Some of you can man the hotline from your home. You won't even need to work in our office. And those of you who like to shop can be Mystery Shoppers, checking out the stores—even the flea markets—in our town for suspicious business practices."

Edna suddenly sat upright and blurted out,

"Buckler's Bloodhounds! That's a much better name than the one you cops thought up. It's got a snap to it."

"She's a pest!" Jose shouted at the officer. "Argues about everything. She's a pain in the neck. Don't pay any attention to her. We didn't come to hear Edna. We came to hear you."

Gladys stood up, looked back and forth from the officer to Jose, as if she were at a tennis match following the ball. "Please don't start an argument again, Jose. Edna may be right. I like the name she thought up. If we're going to go sniffing out fraud, then Bloodhounds isn't a bad name. Buckler's Bloodhounds. I do like it."

"So do I," Olivia said. "Maybe the six of us could call ourselves Buckler's Bloodhounds."

Officer Martin smiled. "We're just setting up our plan. The name for our project isn't carved in stone. I like Buckler's Bloodhounds too." She beamed at Mrs. Merkel, as if she were a child who had stopped being naughty, and said, "Thank you for thinking up such a great name."

Abbie expected Mrs. Merkel to give a rude answer, but instead she turned around and smiled at everyone in the group, enjoying the praise, seemingly thrilled at having her idea accepted. Abbie surprised herself by feeling a sudden pang of sympathy for Mrs. Merkel. *I didn't realize she feels left out*, she thought. *Maybe if she were nicer to people* . . .

"Usually I'm the only one here who *can* think," Mrs. Merkel added, and Abbie's sympathy vanished.

37

Lawanda hefted herself to her feet. "There's nothin' I like better'n shoppin'," she said. "I want to be a Mystery Shopper."

Officer Martin wrote Lawanda's name on a pad of paper on her clipboard, and everyone announced what they'd be willing to do.

Suddenly Abbie realized that everyone was looking at Mrs. Merkel. When she didn't respond, Jose said, "How about that? Edna the loudmouth's got nothing to say."

"Sure, I've got something to say," Mrs. Merkel answered. "I'm waiting for the lady cop to leave so we can get back to our book club business. Now that I've got a driver, I don't intend to miss a single meeting."

An evil sparkle appeared in Jose's eyes. "I make a motion," he said loudly. "Why don't we disband the book club and use our time to work for the Buckler Bloodhounds?"

Abbie saw him elbow Sam, who added, "I second the motion."

"Oh, my! Then I suppose we'd better vote. All in favor?" Gladys asked.

The ayes were unanimous, except for Edna Merkel.

Olivia put a hand on Mrs. Merkel's shoulder. "I'm sorry you don't want to join us," she said.

Mrs. Merkel angrily shook Olivia's hand away. "Who said I wasn't going to join you? I am. You all remember when I helped the police catch that guy who was parked near the children's playground?"

Jose let out a loud groan, and some of the others looked pained.

"We heard the story," Lawanda said.

"Many times," Dolores added.

Addressing herself to Officer Martin, Mrs. Merkel bragged, "I did just what you said. I kept my eyes and ears open and noticed things. When I saw the same car parked on the street across from the playground with that guy sitting in it, I knew he was up to no good. So I gave his license number and description to the police. When they checked him out, they found he had a record."

"That was good detective work," Officer Martin said. "That's exactly what we want."

"You didn't hear the rest of the story," Jose said. "When the guy got out of his car and walked toward the playground, Edna hit him with her handbag. The police didn't come because of her call, they came because they thought they were stopping a case of assault and battery. She's the one who should have been arrested."

"I was just making a citizen's arrest." Mrs. Merkel sneered at Jose as she added, "I've also had experience turning in illegals." She said to Officer Martin, "It's decided. I'll be a private eye for Buckler's Bloodhounds."

Jose hooted. "There aren't any private eyes in the Bloodhounds."

Officer Martin politely smiled at Mrs. Merkel and said, "We like to think of senior citizen investigators as neighborhood scouts."

"Don't call me a senior citizen," Mrs. Merkel snapped. "That's a label for old people. And what kind of a name is *neighborhood scouts*? Do these scouts also help old ladies cross the street?" She tapped the officer's clipboard. "Write my name on there the way I told you: Edna Merkel, private eye." She glanced scornfully at the others. "I'm not afraid to take on a dangerous job."

Officer Martin took a quick step forward. "Please, let me assure you all, there is no danger in any of the jobs you're asked to do. We don't want you to confront someone who is breaking the law. We simply want information. You know—license number, name of the company contacting you, time, place—you'll be given literature that will explain all that."

Later, after the meeting had disbanded and Abbie was driving Mrs. Merkel home, she asked, "Mr. Morales seems like such a nice person. Why is he so angry with you?"

Mrs. Merkel chuckled gleefully. "Jose and his son have a landscaping service. They have a rapid turnover with their crews, so they get help wherever they can. That means hiring illegal aliens who have sneaked into the country."

Abbie was puzzled. "How do you know they do this?"

"Their crews work in our neighborhood—mow lawns, trim bushes, and all that. I keep a sharp eye out. I remember faces. The law's the law. You can't hire illegals. So twice now I've notified the INS to check them out, and I was right. Jose and his son have had to pay fines. One more time and

40

they're in really big trouble." She looked smug as she added, "Which they may be in again. Their excuse is that they can't get enough U.S. citizens or foreigners with green cards to do the work, but that doesn't matter. I'm not going to let Jose get away with breaking the law."

She deliberately got Jose into trouble, Abbie thought. *And it looks as if she plans to do it again. No wonder he can't stand her.*

As Abbie stopped the car in front of the walkway to Mrs. Merkel's front door, Mrs. Merkel ordered, "Come inside. As my assistant, you'll need to know what to do."

Abbie looked at her watch. "I've been with you all afternoon," she said. "I have to get home to help my mom make dinner and have the car there if she needs it. You know I'm using my mother's car to drive you around."

Mrs. Merkel stubbornly folded her arms across her chest. "Then I'll tell you what you need to know right here," she said.

Abbie sighed, realizing that she was going to have to listen whether she wanted to or not.

"First of all, you can't talk about what you see or hear when you're with me. I wouldn't be surprised if I just might be involved with a major case, and I don't want you spilling the beans to people I'm investigating."

"I'm not going to spill anything. I think you've watched too many old private-eye shows on TV."

"Don't interrupt. Children should be seen and not heard." Mrs. Merkel hurried on. "Your main job will be to drive me where I need to go and

41

make sure I don't misplace any of my equipment."

"What equipment?"

"Don't ask stupid questions. Private-eye equipment. Digital phone, notebook and pen, dark glasses, maybe a camera. Now, tomorrow—"

"Sundays I get off." Remembering what was printed on one of the sheets in her folder, Abbie quickly added, "And on Monday after school the girls who are in the Friend to Friend program will meet with Mrs. Wilhite."

"A lot of good it's going to do me to have *you* for a driver!" Mrs. Merkel complained.

"The meetings are only one Monday a month," Abbie explained.

"I'd say they're one Monday too many. You already know what they expect you to do, so anything else is a waste of time."

Abbie wanted to laugh, realizing that she and Mrs. Merkel had finally agreed on one thing. "I'll see you Tuesday after school," Abbie said. "Would you like me to drive you to the grocery store?"

Mrs. Merkel brightened. "I'd like to go to that big supermarket in the new shopping center," she said. "The store in my neighborhood has a bunch of losers for clerks. They can't get along with anybody."

"I'll see you Tuesday," Abbie said, eager to leave.

Mrs. Merkel nodded before she slowly climbed out of the car. She paused before she closed the door, bending down to look in at Abbie. "Tuesday at three o'clock. Don't be late. No excuses. Besides going grocery shopping, I've got big things in mind. I won't tell you my idea because you'd just blab it to everybody."

The excited flush on Mrs. Merkel's face worried Abbie. "Remember what Officer Martin told you," she said. "The police don't want you to do anything dangerous."

Mrs. Merkel's eyes narrowed. "Maybe I should let that stupid group leader know you're uncooperative."

For an instant Abbie closed her eyes, pretending in the darkness that she could magically cause Mrs. Merkel and Mrs. Wilhite to disappear. She opened her eyes again, half hoping her wish had come true, only to see Mrs. Merkel staring at her.

Abbie sighed. "I'll be here on Tuesday at three o'clock," she said.

CHAPTER FIVE

~~~~~~~~~~~~~~~~~~~~~~~~~~~~~~~~

On Sunday morning after church, Mrs. Thompson drove Abbie and Davy to the Pancake House.

"How come we're here?" Davy asked as he pressed his nose against the car window. "We only eat here on birthdays."

"And special occasions," Mrs. Thompson said, her voice so light and bright that Abbie half expected to see stars float out of her mouth with her words.

"Why is this a special occasion?" Abbie asked. She tried to think what they might be celebrating and came up blank.

"We're celebrating the beginning of more family time together," her mother answered.

44

Davy threw off his seat belt, bouncing on the seat. "You mean Dad will be here too?" he shouted.

Mrs. Thompson sucked in her breath. "No, honey. He won't be here. It will be just you and Abbie and me. We're the family now. And we're going to have fun and do things together and talk—really talk—to each other."

As Mrs. Thompson opened her car door and stepped out, Davy confronted Abbie. His eyes reddened with the tears he was obviously fighting to hold back. "What's with Mom?" he demanded.

Abbie shrugged. "I don't know. Humor her."

Davy's lower lip curled out, and he frowned. "It's because of you."

"Me?"

"Getting arrested. Now Mom's gonna try to be Supermom and drive us crazy, and it's all your fault."

Shocked, Abbie tried to answer, but Davy had jumped out, slamming the door so hard that the car rocked. Abbie got out of the car on the other side and hurried to catch up with her mother, who had crossed the parking lot and was waiting for them in the shade of the restaurant's overhang.

Abbie took a good look at her mother. The breeze from the bay had caught the hem of her pale blue skirt, swirling it around her long legs. Her strawberry-blond hair, which Abbie was glad she'd inherited, gleamed in the late-morning light. For a moment Abbie could see her mother

45

not as a middle-aged woman, fifteen pounds overweight, but as a young woman excited and happy about life. That must have been the way Abbie's father had seen her when they first fell in love.

As Mrs. Thompson stepped inside the air-conditioned restaurant, Abbie caught up with Davy. She gripped his shoulder hard. "Don't do anything to spoil Mom's day, or you're history," she said.

"Quit that," Davy complained. He tried to wriggle free.

Abbie released her grip, but she said, "I mean it. Mom's had a tough time, so be nice to her."

Davy whirled to face her, anger still in his eyes. "*Mom's* had a tough time? What about *us*? What about *me*? Because of her I haven't got a dad around anymore."

"You're wrong!" Abbie cried. "Dad left because he didn't want us. As far as he was concerned, we were nothing. We were nobody. It's not Mom's fault."

"Shut up! That's a big lie! Dad wants us to live with him—I know he does—but Mom won't let us."

Abbie saw the fear and desperation in Davy's eyes. Aching for him, and hating her father even more, she put an arm around Davy's shoulders. "Right now it doesn't matter what you believe or if you're right or wrong. We're all hurting," she said. "Be good to Mom. Okay?"

Davy broke away. He ran to the door of the

restaurant, tugged it open, and disappeared inside.

Soon they were seated, menus in hand. Abbie stared at the words, which became unreadable dark squiggles on the page. She wasn't hungry. She really didn't want pancakes. She didn't want anything more than life as it used to be, and that was impossible.

"Oh, doesn't everything look wonderful?" Mrs. Thompson asked cheerfully. Her voice was so high and brittle Abbie winced, expecting the words to shatter and crash to the floor. "Davy, they've got that Strawberry Tower you like so much."

"I hate Strawberry Towers," Davy grumbled.

Abbie kicked his ankle under the table. He automatically kicked back, and she jumped as his shoe connected with her shin. Behind the menu she glared at him, but he simply looked away, as if he didn't care what she had promised or threatened.

"How about the apple pecan pancakes?" Mrs. Thompson asked, her voice less perky.

Aching for her mother, who was trying much too hard, Abbie said, "Great idea, Mom. That's exactly what I want."

"Davy?" Mrs. Thompson asked.

Someone suddenly stepped between Abbie and Davy, resting his hands on their shoulders. Startled, Abbie quickly glanced up and saw her father.

"Dad!" Davy shouted so joyfully that people nearby turned to look and smile.

"I saw your car outside," Dr. Thompson said. "I thought I'd stop by and say hello." He pulled out the fourth chair at the table and sat down. "I've just moved into a condo two blocks from here. It faces the water and has a place to store my boat. Has a nice view, too."

"Who cares?" Abbie wanted to say, but she clamped her lips together tightly and stared down at her menu. He wouldn't hear if she spoke. She didn't exist. She was a nothing . . . a nobody.

Abbie saw her mother's lips part, as though she intended to speak, but Davy burst in, shouting eagerly, "You've got a boat? Really? Dad, if you've got a boat we could go fishing!"

"Davy, I—"

"Is it a sailboat? Does it have a motor?"

"Yes." Dr. Thompson shot a quick, guilty glance at his wife before he added, "It's just a sixteen-footer. Got it secondhand."

"Wow!" Davy shouted. "Dad! Could I come and live with you?"

Dr. Thompson cleared his throat. "Davy, not—"

Abbie slapped her menu down on the table. She could feel the heat in her face and knew she was blushing. "Be quiet, Davy," she commanded. "You're yelling."

Davy did lower his voice, but he leaned toward his father, clutching his arm. "Could I, Dad? Could I come and live with you? Now? It wouldn't take me long to pack."

Dr. Thompson's forehead puckered, and he

looked at Davy sadly. "We can't talk about that now, son," he said. "Maybe after I'm settled . . . Your mother . . ."

In the silence Abbie watched the expression on her little brother's face twist from joy and excitement to misery. She instinctively stretched out a hand to touch his arm. "It's okay, Davy," she said.

But Davy shrugged her hand away. "Mom won't let me, will she?" he cried, tears running down his cheeks. "Why won't you let me live with Dad, Mom?"

Mrs. Thompson glared at her husband. "That was cute, putting it on me," she said. "Tell him the truth. Tell Davy that the decision to leave us was all yours. Tell him you don't want him around to interfere with your romance."

"Be reasonable, Sandra," Dr. Thompson said.

"Tell him," Mrs. Thompson insisted.

Dr. Thompson pushed back his chair and stood. His back was straight, his expression stern. Abbie could picture him in his intimidating classroom. "Sandra, I stopped by only to give my family a friendly greeting," he said. "I didn't expect you to turn it into an unhappy issue."

Mrs. Thompson spoke slowly. "You coward! Get . . . out . . . of here."

Davy twisted in his chair, trying to grab his father's arm. "Dad, can I go with you? Please?"

Dr. Thompson bent to touch Davy's cheek with his own. "You can't, Davy," he said sadly. "You heard your mother."

As his father strode out of the restaurant, Davy wadded his napkin, shoving it up against his eyes. "I hate you, Mom," he muttered. "I hate you."

Abbie met the gazes of the people who were staring, forcing them to look away. "Mom," she said. "Let's go home. We've got pancake mix in the cupboard. I'll make some pancakes."

Mrs. Thompson gripped the arms of her chair, her face as blotchy as though she'd been slapped. "Yes, Abbie," she whispered. "Let's go home."

Davy refused to eat Abbie's pancakes, and Mrs. Thompson took only two bites before she pushed her plate away. "I'm sorry," she said to Abbie. "Lately I seem to have very little appetite."

As Davy threw open the pantry door and began to cram the pockets of his jacket with packages of peanut butter crackers, Mrs. Thompson asked, "Davy, what are you doing?"

"Getting something to eat," he answered.

"Abbie made you these perfectly good pancakes. She—"

"I hate pancakes. You can't make me eat them. I'm never going to eat pancakes again." He ran to the kitchen door.

"Where are you going?"

"Outside."

"Where outside?"

Davy turned and glared at his mother. "P.J.'s coming over. That's okay, isn't it? I mean, you

50

are going to let me see my best friend, aren't you?"

Mrs. Thompson sighed. "Honey, I wish you'd try to understand. If you'd like, we could find a quiet place to talk."

Davy didn't answer. He raced out the kitchen door, slamming it behind him.

In misery Abbie watched a tear roll down her mother's cheek. Another followed and another. She stared down at the wedding ring on her hand, not moving, not even seeming to notice she was crying. Abbie got up, pulled a fistful of tissues from the box on the kitchen counter, and handed them to her.

"Mom," she said, "let's go to a movie this afternoon. Okay?"

When Abbie didn't get an answer she kept talking, realizing she was babbling but unable to stop. "We can see that new sci-fi film. Davy will like that one. I mean, all the kids are talking about it, and he hasn't seen it yet. That ought to make him feel better. Oh, I mean, you know—distract him. We could even take P.J. with us and stop off afterward for hamburgers. Want me to call P.J.'s mom?"

Mrs. Thompson leaned back in her chair and mopped at her eyes and nose with the tissues. "If it's okay with you, Abbie, I really don't feel like a movie today. You can ask Gigi over if you'd like to."

"Gigi and her family are driving to Corpus Christi to visit her grandmother. I'd like to do something with you, Mom. Really, I would."

"Davy doesn't understand . . ."

Abbie patted her mother's shoulder. "I know, Mom. But he will."

"I should take him to counseling, but right now I can't afford it."

Mrs. Thompson got to her feet, gave Abbie a hug, and left the kitchen.

The telephone rang, and Abbie reached for it eagerly. Maybe Gigi hadn't gone out of town.

"Hi, Abbie," a deep, soft voice said. "This is Nick Campos."

Abbie stood silently, her mouth open, and Nick went on. "Remember me? English class?"

"Y-Yes," Abbie said. Of course she remembered Nick. He was tall, with dark curly hair and deep brown eyes. Nick was fun and good-looking.

"I was wondering if you were free to go to a movie with me this afternoon," he said.

Abbie was startled and confused by her mixed-up feelings. Nick was a nice guy and had a great smile. But Dad had a great smile too, and what was behind it? A man who would walk out of the lives of his wife and children as if they didn't matter.

Abbie gripped the phone. She cleared her throat, when her voice didn't seem to be working, and tried to speak up. "I'm sorry, Nick. It was nice of you to ask me, but I can't go out today. I've got . . . other stuff to do."

"I shouldn't have called so late," Nick said. "It's just that it's such a pretty day, and I got to thinking about you, and . . . well . . . can I call you again for a date, Abbie?"

"Yes," Abbie said, wishing she had said no.

Nick said goodbye, and Abbie echoed the word. She slowly hung up the receiver. Probably at any other time of her life a call from a cute guy like Nick would have thrilled her. Upset by her feelings, she grew even angrier at her father.

As she cleaned the kitchen, Abbie tried not to think about him. Every time he came to mind her stomach clutched and pain tightened her chest.

Sunday's *Buckler Bee* still lay folded on one end of the table. Abbie sat at the table and spread the newspaper flat. The headline dominated the top half of the first page: BANK PRESIDENT SHOT. Below the headline, next to the news story, were two large color photos. One was a fairly recent shot of Delmar Hastings with his wife and children. The other was a studio portrait of the bank's head cashier, Irene Conley.

"So that's who Irene Conley is," Abbie said aloud. She had seen Irene working in the bank but hadn't known either her name or her job. The picture flattered her. Blond hair, green eyes, mouth just a little too wide—the real-life Irene didn't have the softness of features that the camera had given her.

Abbie read the story but didn't learn much more than she had from the group of senior citizens. "At seven-fifteen A.M. Saturday an unknown person or persons robbed the Gulf East Savings and Loan. The head cashier had been knocked unconscious, the president of the bank had been shot and killed, and the vault was found open. No estimate has yet been made as to the amount of the missing money."

As she thought about the crime, Abbie felt a wave of sorrow not only for Mr. Hastings and his family, but also for Irene Conley. How horrible it must have been for her to come back to consciousness and find her employer dead.

Abbie studied the picture of the Hastings children. The youngest boy looked close to her age. *You lost a father too,* she thought, *but at least you know that your father didn't want to leave you. He wasn't like mine.* With a shudder, Abbie quickly turned the page of the newspaper.

Beside her the telephone rang. Her mind still on her father, Abbie angrily gripped the receiver. *If this is Dad,* she thought, *I'm going to tell him exactly what I think of him for butting in and spoiling Mom's day.*

"Hello," she yelled at the phone.

"Don't yell like that. Keep your voice down, or you're going to ruin everything."

"Mrs. Merkel?"

"Of course it's me. You shouldn't have to ask."

Abbie took a deep breath and answered with satisfaction, "It's Sunday, Mrs. Merkel. I have the day off."

"Day off? What kind of an assistant are you? Days off are for people with nine-to-five jobs, not for private investigators. I need you. Right away."

"I can't."

Mrs. Merkel lowered her voice. "They're on my block now, you stupid girl."

"Who's on your block?"

"The crooks. Who else?"

"But—"

"Don't argue. Is Mrs. Wilhite going to tell me you have Sundays off when I tell her I asked you for help and you refused to come?"

"Look, Mrs. Merkel," Abbie said. "I'm not going to let you intimidate me. If I get in trouble with Mrs. Wilhite, well, okay. So be it. Just because you tell me that crooks are on your block, you expect me to—"

A recorded message suddenly interrupted Abbie. "If you wish to place a call, please hang up and dial again."

Abbie slammed down the phone. "Crazy old lady!" she grumbled. "She hung up on me."

Mrs. Thompson appeared in the doorway, raw hope in her eyes. "Was that call for me?" she asked.

Abbie groaned. *It wasn't Dad, if that's what you're asking,* she thought. *Oh, Mom, don't hope that he'll call you. Don't expect him to. He isn't going to apologize for what he did. He isn't going to beg you to take him back. Not ever.*

"It was Mrs. Merkel," Abbie answered. "She's worried about some crooks."

"Crooks? What is she talking about?"

"I don't know, Mom," Abbie said, "but I'd better drive over to her house. Could I use the car?"

"Sure," Mrs. Thompson said.

The phone rang again, and Abbie picked it up. She turned away so that she couldn't see the spark of hope on her mother's face.

"Get over here fast!" Mrs. Merkel yelled into the phone. "Those crooks are coming closer. They're practically next door."

CHAPTER SIX

~~~~~~~~~~~~~~~~

bbie scanned Darnell Street as she drove onto Mrs. Merkel's block. A tar-encrusted black truck and a small trailer with roofing equipment stood on the street in front of Mrs. Merkel's home.

Abbie parked her car a short distance away and walked to Mrs. Merkel's house. She could see two men, their overalls as dirty as their truck, leaving the porch of the house next to Mrs. Merkel's.

As she reached to press Mrs. Merkel's doorbell, the door flew open and a gnarled hand shot out. Mrs. Merkel grabbed Abbie's arm, pulling her into the house, and slammed the door.

Abbie squinted in the dim light, examining

her surroundings. The room was tidy, but the furniture was old, its faded, stiff plush fabric a reminder that it must have been new in the forties. Crocheted doilies covered the chair arms, and inexpensive little figurines and knickknacks rested on a built-in bookcase. A foot-high Asian bronze horse with inset eyes of gleaming black stone stood, one front leg raised, on a teak pedestal at one end of a coffee table. The kind of oversweet, floral scent that comes from a spray can hung in the air, and yellowed lace curtains at the windows filtered out most of the sunlight. Abbie noticed that there weren't any framed photographs, even though they seemed to belong in this setting.

Mrs. Merkel leaned back against the door. "Did you see those men?" she asked. "They've been in Buckler before, over on the next street— Effie Glebe's house. *Said* they were roofers. Ha! Tore up her roof. Put some gunk on it that leaked bad at the first rain. And I'd hate to tell you what a terrible high price they charged her. Effie filed a complaint, but by that time they were long gone from Buckler and the police couldn't find them. Now they're back—the same people. What a nerve. They think they can pull the same thing again and get away with it. I got a good look at them last fall, and I don't forget things like that. They've even got the same truck. They didn't know that they'd tangle with me."

Abbie nodded. "I guess you should report them to Buckler's Bloodhounds."

Mrs. Merkel chuckled. "I'll report them, all

right. That's why I needed you to be here. You're my witness."

The doorbell rang so suddenly that both Abbie and Mrs. Merkel jumped.

Mrs. Merkel tiptoed to the nearest front window and held back the curtain a half inch to peek through. "It's them," she said. "You sit over here behind the door, where they can't see you. You can watch them through the crack in the door. Just remember to keep quiet and pay attention. I'll do all the talking."

The chair she had put behind the door was a lightweight wooden one that looked as if it could be an antique. Abbie sat on it carefully, thankful that it didn't wobble.

Mrs. Merkel opened her door and sternly asked, "Yes?"

Abbie looked through the crack in the door, as Mrs. Merkel had ordered her to do. She did have a good view—across the porch and all the way to the street. Facing her were two very dissimilar men. The tall one was husky and muscular, with at least two days' growth of beard on his face. The shorter one was thin and small-boned. Their clothes were stained with tar.

The husky man stepped forward, gripping a clipboard and pen. "I'm Mitchell, with the All-Round Roofing Company," he said. "We had work in your neighborhood and couldn't help noticing how bad your roof looks. It needs work."

"My late husband said our roof would last forty years," Mrs. Merkel told him.

"Nobody's roof lasts that long," Mitchell said.

He shook his head sadly. "We can beat the competition and give you a good, fair price. How about we do this—" he turned to the other man. "Eddie, you just run up there and take a close look at what's wrong." To Mrs. Merkel he said, "I'll walk around your house. I need to examine the joints and gutters."

Eddie shot away, pulled a ladder from the truck, stuffed something from the truck into his pockets, and was soon on the roof of Mrs. Merkel's house. Abbie could hear him thumping around and hoped he wouldn't fall through.

Still in the doorway, Mrs. Merkel turned to Abbie and grinned. "I've got a perfectly good composition roof with ten years to go on the warranty. It's going to be mighty interesting to hear what they have to report."

It didn't take long for both men to return. Mitchell came up the steps to the porch, sadly shaking his head. "Sorry to tell you this," he said, "but your roof needs major repair work."

Eddie held out some ragged, worn scraps of composition. "Take a look. Your roof is falling apart."

Mrs. Merkel reached out for the piece of composition, examined it, and dropped it into a pocket in her skirt. She sighed and said, "What's it going to cost me?"

Mitchell coolly named a figure. The number seemed so high that Abbie was astounded. Was that what it cost to fix a roof?

"I don't know what to do," Mrs. Merkel said.

"That seems like an awful lot of money. Maybe I better call around."

"Tell you what," Mitchell went on. "Today being Sunday, we've got time to take care of most of the problems right now. If you agree to let us get going with the job today and pay in advance—we take checks—I'll take ten percent off the total price and you'll get our standard contract. It also includes a lifetime warranty." He held out the clipboard. "You can sign right here."

"Fill it out first," Mrs. Merkel said. "I want to see everything in writing before I sign it or write a check."

She waited until he handed her the contract, then smiled again. "I'll just close the door while I get my checkbook," she said. "Don't start fixing anything until I come back."

"They broke your roof," Abbie whispered as Mrs. Merkel strode past her to a little desk.

"No, they didn't," Mrs. Merkel said quietly. "That isn't part of my roof. Didn't you see Eddie slip something into his pocket when he went to the truck?"

"Oh," Abbie said. "Yes, I did, but I didn't think—"

"That's the trouble with you. You didn't think. Well, I did, and this piece I've got is evidence. Now you know why I'm a private eye and you're not." She picked up one of the cards Officer Martin had handed out and dialed the phone. She identified herself and said, "Officer Martin, I need the police. There are two crooks on my front porch who tried to pull a scam on me."

There was a pause while Mrs. Merkel listened to what Officer Martin had to say. Then Mrs. Merkel vigorously shook her head. "If you won't come, I'll make a citizen's arrest. I'll—" She looked at Abbie. "No, I'm not alone. My driver is with me. You met her at the meeting. She's a witness to everything those con men said and did."

She smiled into the phone. "I knew you'd see it my way. I'll see you in a few minutes."

As Mrs. Merkel hung up, Abbie asked, "Why don't you just do what the Buckler's Bloodhounds are supposed to do? Report in and let the police take over."

Mrs. Merkel shook her head. "By the time the police checked things out and found the papers on Effie's complaint, those two buzzards would be long gone again. It's better to do this my way."

She stuffed the roofer's agreement and the scrap of roofing material in a desk drawer and went back to the door. "No check," she said as she opened it. "I thought you two looked familiar when I saw your truck, so I called some friends of mine. You think you can pull a scam on me?"

Mrs. Merkel stepped out on the porch. "You two scam artists claimed to fix Effie Glebe's roof last year, and you wrecked it. She filed a complaint with the police, and they went looking for you. But you left Buckler so they couldn't find you. Hit and run. That's the way you operate."

Mitchell stood his ground. Abbie saw him look at Eddie. Eddie barely nodded, then began to move behind Mrs. Merkel. He put out an arm, and the front door swung wide open.

Abbie's heart pounded so loudly she was afraid Eddie could hear it. Quietly she got to her feet.

Through the crack in the door she could see Mitchell move closer to Mrs. Merkel, forcing her to step back.

"What do you think you're doing?" Mrs. Merkel demanded.

"Let's go inside and talk," Mitchell ordered. "You said your *late* husband. We won't be bothering anyone."

"You're not welcome in my house. Besides, the police will be here any minute."

Eddie said, "That's what they say in old detective movies." He backed into the room, standing beside the open door.

Abbie knew that Mitchell couldn't see around the door. And Eddie didn't know she was standing behind him. Even though she was so frightened that her arms shook, she picked up the chair and jammed the base of one of the narrow legs into the middle of Eddie's back. "Put your hands up and keep them up," she said sternly.

Eddie did as he was told. "Don't shoot!" he whimpered.

Abbie tried to put a snarl in her voice. "Then tell your partner he'd better not move an inch until the police get here."

"M-Mitchell?" Eddie's voice shook. "Did you hear her?"

"I heard. Who's back there? Who are you?"

"Never you mind," Mrs. Merkel snapped. "There's the squad car now."

Mitchell growled, "You're going to be sorry you did this, lady."

"Huh! You don't scare me," Mrs. Merkel said.

Officer Martin and her partner—a tall, lanky man who unsnapped his holster as he ran up the walk—took charge. Mrs. Merkel quickly described how Mitchell and Eddie had tried to force her into the house, thinking she was alone.

The two men were handcuffed and put into the back of the squad car. Then Officer Martin returned to Mrs. Merkel's front porch. She was no longer the polite public speaker who had visited the senior citizens' book club. Her eyes flashed with irritation.

"Your actions endangered not only your own life, but this girl's life too."

"We weren't in danger. We can take care of ourselves."

"You also endangered our program. It's set up so that senior citizens help protect other senior citizens. We can't have them confronting crooks and putting their own lives in danger. Do you understand me, Mrs. Merkel?"

Mrs. Merkel lifted her chin and held it out stubbornly. "I understand whatever I need to understand," she said.

"Then no more playing cops and robbers." Officer Martin's voice softened. "Thank you for pinpointing these con men. We'd like you to come down to headquarters and file a complaint as soon as you can."

When Officer Martin had left, Mrs. Merkel shut her front door and leaned against it. "Since that snippy little cop doesn't want my help, she's not going to get it on the big stuff."

"What? She thanked you. She said—"

"I handed over a pair of perps to Miss High and Mighty and she scolded me. She'll take all the credit for making the collar, and I did all the work. I made sure those perps would take the rap for what they did to Effie."

Abbie couldn't help it. She began to giggle.

Mrs. Merkel scowled. "What's so funny?"

"I feel like I'm in an old movie."

Mrs. Merkel's frown grew deeper. "There's nothing to laugh about. That's the way detectives and private eyes talk. If you went to Paris, you'd try to speak French, wouldn't you?"

Abbie sank back into one of the overstuffed chairs, stretching her legs out in front of her. None of what was happening made sense.

"Don't think you can settle in there," Mrs. Merkel told her. "I have to admit you did okay with that chair, but we're not through. Drive me to the police station. We've got unfinished business to take care of."

----

CHAPTER SEVEN

s Abbie turned the corner from Darnell onto Main, Mrs. Merkel stiffened. She pointed to a small strip shopping center in the next block and said, "Pull in there. Hurry up. And pay attention to that van at the intersection."

Abbie drove into the parking lot and pulled up in front of a small grocery store. "I thought you wanted to go to the supermarket," she said. She took the key from the ignition and reached for the door handle.

"Don't open that door!" Mrs. Merkel ordered.

"What?"

"I didn't say I wanted to go *inside* the store. I just told you to park. I can see what I want to see from here." Mrs. Merkel opened her large handbag and put on her sunglasses. She next pulled out a small green leather notebook, turned to a clean page, and jotted down some numbers and letters. "Gotcha!" she exclaimed.

"Was that a license number?" Abbie asked.

"Yes," Mrs. Merkel said. "See that guy in the dusty gray sedan parked over there? He's waiting for somebody to make a cellular phone call."

Abbie stared at Mrs. Merkel, puzzled. "How do you know that?"

"I know because I read a lot, I know what's going on, and I can figure things out, which is a lot more than I can say about most people—including you."

"I still don't get why you wrote down his license number," Abbie said. "Won't you tell me?"

"Why should I?" Mrs. Merkel rummaged through her handbag and pulled out a digital phone.

Mrs. Merkel dialed a number, and when someone answered she said, "My name is Edna Merkel, and I want to talk to Officer Martin."

There was a pause, and Mrs. Merkel added, "That's for Officer Martin to find out. I talk to her and no one else. Understand?"

In less than a minute Mrs. Merkel said, "Officer Martin, I want you to arrest someone. I've written down his description, his car's description, and his license number." She read the information from her notebook.

Abbie could guess what Officer Martin responded, because Mrs. Merkel said, "Of course I have a reason for wanting him arrested. Haven't people in Buckler complained enough about their cell phone numbers being used to make drug calls, with the bills going to them? The whole story was in the paper just two weeks ago."

Smugly she continued, "Well, you can thank me for catching him for you. On two days last week his car was parked opposite one of the phone company's stores. The store's been running a two-week special, and it's full of customers, so he's there again. His car is dirty and gray—the kind that doesn't stand out, so he thinks no one will notice what he's up to. He doesn't stay long, but while he's there, every now and then he perks up and writes something down."

"How do you know all this?" Abbie blurted out.

"Don't interrupt," Mrs. Merkel snapped. She scowled. "No, Officer Martin. I wasn't talking to you. I was talking to my driver."

Mrs. Merkel turned her back on Abbie and continued her story. "Everybody knows that when you buy a cell phone the company does whatever they have to do to activate it. Then they tell you to make one free courtesy call, just to make sure the phone's working okay. You follow me, don't you?"

Without waiting for an answer, Mrs. Merkel continued. "I'm sure this guy I've seen has been picking up each call with his equipment, getting the cell phone number, and writing it down. Then he either gives his list of numbers to a contact or sells it. Doesn't matter which. What matters is that he's there in front of the store right now, and if you move on it, you can nab him. But you'd better get here fast."

"How did you find out all that information about picking up cell phone numbers?" Abbie asked as Mrs. Merkel ended the conversation and tucked her phone away.

"I told you, I read a lot. There are news stories every once in a while about people driving slow past houses, trying to catch a cell phone in use. They can get the numbers easy and then make a lot of long distance calls using them. So why shouldn't a crook figure out just what I did, that it would be even easier to just park across from a store that's doing a booming business in selling cell phones and offering free calls?"

"You really are good at figuring things out," Abbie said in wonder. "Did you ever actually work for the police?"

"Work for the police? Ha!" Mrs. Merkel exclaimed.

Before Mrs. Merkel could launch into a diatribe against the police, Abbie asked, "Did your husband? Did you learn police tactics from him?"

Mrs. Merkel turned to face Abbie, who imagined she could feel the woman's glare drilling into her forehead. "What I learned from my husband was to never trust a man—especially one who started out full of sweet talk and flattery and pretty gifts he sent me from foreign ports. The day he walked out on me I was through with him forever, and that includes answering stupid questions about him. Never ask me about him again. You hear me?"

"I hear you," Abbie said, "and I'm sorry I asked. I didn't know." Trying to make amends, she said, "I know how rough that must have been on you and your children."

"We never had children," Mrs. Merkel answered. "The only kin I've got is a good-for-nothing lazy nephew from his side of the family. Charlie Merkel is almost as worthless as his uncle was. But he does come down from Dallas a couple of times a year to patch up things around my house. He tells me he wants to see how I am and help out if he can, but I know what he's after.

"Last time he was here he tried to borrow money—as if I'd be stupid enough to let him have any. If he runs up debts, that's his problem. Charlie will be my heir since he's the only relative, so he can darned well wait until he inherits my money someday."

She cackled and added, "It'll serve him right if I outlive him—which I intend to do."

As a police car entered the parking lot, Mrs. Merkel shouted to Abbie, "Quick! Park in front of the crook! Block him off on this side!"

"What if he has a gun?"

"Do what I tell you!"

No sooner had Abbie driven to face the gray sedan, nearly touching its bumper, than Mrs. Merkel jumped from the car.

She arrived at the window of the sedan only a few seconds ahead of one of the police officers.

"Gotcha, you stupid crook!" Mrs. Merkel yelled at the man in the car.

The officer glared at her. "Move out of the way, ma'am," he ordered.

"I want him to know that he wins the Stupid Crook of the Day award," she shouted back.

"Move, *now!*" the officer commanded as the man in the car yelled obscene threats at Mrs. Merkel.

The second officer took Mrs. Merkel's arm and led her back to Abbie's car. "Pull back," he said to Abbie. "Get your car away from here. You're hampering the police."

Abbie was only too glad to comply. The threats the man had shouted, and his terrible anger, were scary. Not even waiting for Mrs. Merkel to fasten her seat belt, she drove out of the parking lot and into the street.

Mrs. Merkel opened her window and stuck her head out. "He's out of the car," she reported to Abbie. "He's leaning against it, his hands on the car. They're patting him down, looking for weapons."

A smug, satisfied smile on her face, Mrs. Merkel sat back against the seat, fastened her seat belt, and rolled up the window. "Three crooks in one day," she said. "I bet most private eyes don't have records as good as that."

Suddenly she sat up straight, glancing to the right and left. "Where are you going?" she asked.

"I'm taking you home," Abbie said.

"I don't want to go home. I want to go to the police station and sign that complaint." Mrs.

Merkel chuckled. "And see the looks on their faces when I remind them I'm better at nabbing crooks than they are. Then, after that, I want you to drive me to the supermarket in the mall."

Abbie shot a quick glance at Mrs. Merkel. "You're not too tired?"

Sarcastically Mrs. Merkel answered, "No, I'm not too tired. And stop treating me like I'm old and decrepit."

They rode in silence for a few minutes before Mrs. Merkel grumbled, loudly enough for Abbie to hear, "What I *am* tired of are these stupid, lamebrain girls Mrs. Wilhite keeps sending me. I ought to fire this one too."

"Mrs. Merkel," Abbie said quietly, "I'm trying very hard to do whatever you ask me to do . . . even if I don't always agree with your ideas."

"Nobody asked you to agree. You don't have the right to agree or disagree. You're nothing but my driver. That's all." She turned toward Abbie, and once again her stare seemed to drill into Abbie's head. "At least those other girls were model students. You're different. I was warned that you're undisciplined, heading for sure trouble, and if you gave me any trouble I was to send you back."

Abbie flinched. The words were as hurtful as sharp stones. "Who told you that?" she asked. "Mrs. Wilhite?"

"Never you mind. It's none of your business," Mrs. Merkel said. "Only reason I told you is that you need to know just where you stand. Now, watch out up ahead. That light is going to turn red any second."

Abbie gripped the steering wheel. She wanted to cry out against the unfairness of what Mrs. Wilhite had done to her.

"Yes, ma'am," Abbie answered politely. But she thought, *You can be as mean and disagreeable as you want to be, Mrs. Merkel, and I won't care. You think you're so smart and tough? Well, I can be even smarter and tougher.*

Abbie could feel Mrs. Merkel's surprise at her quick agreement. "The police station's right up ahead," Abbie said, "and yes, I do see that truck coming."

CHAPTER EIGHT

----

bbie didn't sleep well Sunday night. She
dreaded going to school the next morning. A
story of her arrest and the action behind it had
appeared in the *Buckler Bee*. She knew how fast
information could spread in Buckler. A lot of the
kids would have read the story—or heard an
even more gossip-glorified version of it.

Just as she'd suspected, as she walked to her
locker a few kids turned away, whispering to each
other. But others took her hand or patted her
shoulder.

"Hang in there, Abbie," Rosa Madrina told
her. "You only did what a lot of us would have
liked to do. I haven't seen my dad for three
years."

Nick Campos suddenly stood before her. Did he know about what had happened? He'd never said a word. "Second try," Nick told her. "On Friday my dad's company is having their annual company picnic at Blue Water Beach. Tons of stuff to eat, swimming, good beach, even a combo and dancing at that Oriental Gardens restaurant. Want to come, Abbie? I really wish you would. We didn't get to know each other very well last year, but I think we'd have fun together."

Abbie leaned against the cold metal of her locker. The chill seemed to spread through her back and neck until her entire body felt like an icicle. The Oriental Gardens at Blue Water Beach had been a favorite with her family. She and Davy had always enjoyed the lavish fountain in the lobby. Its rim was covered with little statues, brass and clay horses and replicas of small villages, with a multitude of tiny dolls dressed in kimonos and fishermen's garb.

Nick's smile warmed his eyes, but she couldn't look beyond them. She liked Nick. But what if she began to like him too much? She didn't want to be hurt.

"Gosh, I'm sorry, Nick," she said. "We've got some family thing for next weekend." She looked away, uncomfortable with the lie she had told. "I really would have liked to go with you. Really."

"My grandmother has an old saying: Third time's the charm," Nick said. "Maybe next time you'll agree to go out with me."

Abbie tried to smile. "Maybe," she said.

What's the matter with me? she wondered as Nick walked away. *Why am I so afraid?*

Gigi joined Abbie at their lockers, which were side by side. "How's your Friend to Friend sweet old lady?" Gigi asked.

"Anything but sweet. She keeps trying to catch crooks."

"Are you serious?"

"Dead serious. Mrs. Merkel thinks she's a private eye." Abbie filled Gigi in on all that had happened.

Gigi laughed so hard she had to lean against the lockers. "I hope the elderly friend they assign to me isn't that wild."

Abbie gaped in surprise. "You aren't in Friend to Friend."

"Yes, I am," Gigi said. "I called Mrs. Wilhite and signed up. All she needs is my transcript and a letter from the school counselor to prove I'm a so-called model student, and I'll bring those to the meeting this afternoon."

Abbie could only blink, shaking her head in disbelief.

"You were really down when I talked to you," Gigi said. "You dreaded going through this by yourself, so here I am. What are friends for?"

Suddenly Abbie's vision was blurred by tears. "You'd do this for me?"

"For you and for some dear, elderly darling. I haven't met her yet, but I know what she's like. She's way overweight, and a hundred years old, and giggles when she talks, and munches on chocolates, and—"

76

Abbie chimed in. "And wears some kind of sweet perfume that smells like marshmallows."

"Don't forget the hat with the sunflower," Gigi added, and they laughed again.

Suddenly the world seemed a much better place to Abbie. If Gigi was at her side during the Friend to Friend meeting, she could live through it, Mrs. Wilhite notwithstanding.

"I've got the car today," Gigi said. "I've already told your mother I'll drive you to and from the meeting so you don't have to use her car."

Somehow Abbie managed to live through the school day, even getting a "Good answer, Abbie," from Mr. Anderson in world history.

Still, long before she was emotionally ready to face Mrs. Wilhite and the other kids in Friend to Friend, Abbie found herself walking with Gigi into a meeting room inside the county courthouse.

There were about two dozen girls in the room and only one adult—a tall, slender woman dressed in an expensive knit suit.

Clutching Gigi's hand, Abbie walked directly to Mrs. Wilhite and introduced herself. Then she introduced Gigi.

Mrs. Wilhite graciously accepted the transcript and recommendation from the school counselor that Gigi handed her. She scanned them, murmured approvingly, then smiled at Gigi.

Mrs. Wilhite suddenly turned to Abbie. "How are you getting along with Mrs. Merkel?" she asked.

"Fine," Abbie answered.

Mrs. Wilhite looked surprised. "You aren't having any problems?"

Abbie looked right into Mrs. Wilhite's eyes. *You just think you're winning*, she thought. She forced herself to look pleasant. "No problems at all," she answered. "Thank you for matching me with Mrs. Merkel. She's a fascinating person."

Unable to cover her surprise, Mrs. Wilhite asked, "You find Mrs. Merkel fascinating?"

"Oh, yes," Abbie said. "Of course you know she has a very quick mind. She's not only interested in book discussions, she's quite active in Buckler's Bloodhounds. She named the group, in fact. Buckler's Bloodhounds. Isn't that clever?"

One of the girls standing next to Mrs. Wilhite asked, "What in the world are Buckler's Bloodhounds?"

Abbie replied, "They're a group of senior citizens who are aiding the police in protecting other seniors against the con men who target them."

"Well," Mrs. Wilhite answered. "I—I hadn't heard of the program." She seemed to struggle to collect herself, then announced loudly, "Girls, will you all find chairs, please? We'll begin our meeting."

Gigi nudged Abbie as they walked toward a pair of empty folding chairs. "If I hadn't been so angry with Mrs. Wilhite I would have burst out laughing. Did you see her face?"

Abbie began to answer, but a short, chubby girl, her eyes crinkled in a smile, touched her arm, interrupting. "Abbie," she said. "My name is Leslie Hodges. Don't let Mrs. Wilhite give you a bad time. Welcome to our group."

Abbie realized her mouth was open. "Thanks, but didn't Mrs. Wilhite tell you about me?"

"Oh, sure. She's a strict straight arrow," Leslie answered. "But who hasn't done something that later they wish they hadn't?" As Mrs. Wilhite rapped on a lectern for order, Leslie quickly said, "I was assigned to Mrs. Merkel until she 'fired' me. So was Joyce Reamer. You seem to be a lot better than we were at dealing with her. Good for you."

"Girls, *please* come to order," Mrs. Wilhite said.

Abbie, Gigi, and Leslie quickly took their seats. The room quieted, and Mrs. Wilhite began to conduct her meeting.

Gigi was given her packet and asked to contact her Friend to Friend assignment during the next two or three days. A few people had questions, which Mrs. Wilhite answered. Then she asked each member to stand as she called her name in alphabetical order and briefly describe an activity she had carried out with the elderly woman assigned to her.

One by one the girls talked about various activities, from inviting their Friends home for dinner to taking them to the park, the grocery store, or choir practice.

Finally Mrs. Wilhite called, "Abbie Thompson."

Nervously Abbie stood and faced the others. How could she tell them that Mrs. Merkel had trapped two roof repair scam artists and led the police to a man stealing cell phone numbers?

She skirted the direct question about what she and Mrs. Merkel had done and began describing Buckler's Bloodhounds. Finally she said, "That's it, I guess," and looked at Mrs. Wilhite.

Mrs. Wilhite cleared her throat and said, "Everyone, please maintain the fine image of our important group. If there is no further business, this meeting is adjourned."

Some of the girls left the meeting room as quickly as possible, but Abbie waited a moment until Leslie had gathered her books. "Thanks for . . . for everything," Abbie said.

"I was ten when my parents divorced," Leslie said. "I still remember how angry I was."

"My brother's ten," Abbie told her. "He's angry all the time. He's even angry at me, and none of what Dad did is my fault."

Leslie nodded. "You have to be patient," she said. "Looking back, I wonder how my mom put up with me." She swung her book bag over her shoulder as she added, "If Mrs. Merkel's working on protecting senior citizens, let your brother in on it. Kids like the game of being spies or detectives. You know."

Abbie nodded. "Thanks," she said. "I'll try it." She couldn't tell Leslie—she couldn't tell anyone—that Mrs. Merkel wasn't following the rules of investigating. And she wasn't involved in a game. She was playing for keeps.

Abbie made macaroni and cheese for dinner because it was Davy's favorite. He came banging in the kitchen door just before their mother was due home from work, tossing his baseball glove, bat, and ball on the floor with a clatter.

Normally Abbie would have yelled at him to stop making so much noise and put his stuff where it belonged. Instead she said, "Davy, I need some help."

"I'm not going to set the table, if that's what you want," he said. "You can do it yourself."

Abbie shook her head. "It hasn't got anything to do with setting the table. I'm worried about some criminals I might have to deal with—some dangerous criminals."

Davy stopped halfway across the room and turned to look at her. "That's dumb," he said, but Abbie knew she had his full attention. "Where would *you* meet a dangerous criminal?"

Abbie lowered her voice and glanced from side to side. "It's a long story," she said. "And it's top secret. Maybe I shouldn't tell you."

Davy plopped into a kitchen chair. "Tell me," he said. "I won't tell anybody."

So Abbie sat opposite him, resting her elbows on the table, and told him about Buckler's Bloodhounds and what Mrs. Merkel had done to catch the con men.

Davy listened, his eyes wide. When Abbie had finished, he said, "You stuck a chair leg into the

81

guy's back and he thought it was a gun? What a turkey! But, hey, that's cool!"

"I don't know what to do," Abbie said. "Mrs. Merkel is really into this private-eye stuff, and she keeps hinting at something big. It's probably all in her imagination, but I'm not sure. What do you think I should do, Davy?"

Davy's forehead wrinkled as he thought a moment. Finally he looked up. "You said she writes things in a little notebook?"

"Yes, but she won't let me see what she writes."

"That's okay. It doesn't matter. You should keep a notebook too."

"What would I write in it?"

"Things like when you meet with her. Put down the day and the times. You know, all that stuff you need to record."

"Hmmm, I don't know what to—"

"Look," Davy interrupted as he shifted impatiently in his chair, "I'll keep it for you. You just report to me every time you've gone to visit her, and if she's done any detecting, then I'll write down what I just told you. Then you can tell me what went on, and I'll write that down too."

Abbie smiled. "Thanks, Davy. I hadn't thought of that."

"I could even come along," Davy suggested, and Abbie relished seeing her brother the way he used to be—happy and interested and excited about something new. She owed Leslie. When she saw her at the next meeting she'd thank her again.

"It's better if Mrs. Merkel doesn't know about you," Abbie said. "She might get suspicious. You could be kind of like—what do they call it?"

"I could go undercover," Davy answered.

"That's it, undercover."

"Yeah!"

Abbie gave an involuntary shiver as she thought of the roofers' faces and the scowl of the man in the gray car. To help Davy she was making a game of the whole thing, and it wasn't a game.

"Stay here. Don't go away. I'll come right back," Davy said. He jumped from the chair, nearly toppling it, and ran from the room.

In just a few minutes he was back, a thin three-hole notebook in his hands. "I took out last year's science project that was in this notebook and put in some clean paper," he said. "This will be our official notebook."

Abbie placed one hand on the notebook. When Davy caught on to what she was doing, he put his hand on her own. She covered it with her other hand, and Davy laid his right hand on top of the pile. "This is our secret notebook," Abbie said solemnly. "You and I are the only ones who will ever read what is in this."

"Right," Davy said.

"You must keep it in a hidden, secret place and guard it with your life."

"Right." Davy thought a moment, then grinned. "I know just where," he said.

As they sat back, he opened the book and began to write. "I'm putting down what you told me," he said. "And then I'll hide the book where no one will find it." He looked at Abbie. "When are you going to visit Mrs. Merkel again?"

"Tomorrow, after school," Abbie said.

"What's she going to do?"

"I have no idea," Abbie answered. She sighed. "I only wish I knew so I could be prepared."

Davy looked eager. "Do you think it will be dangerous?"

"I hope not," Abbie said, but she shivered again. There was no telling what Mrs. Merkel would decide to do.

CHAPTER NINE

"It's about time," Mrs. Merkel snapped as Abbie showed up at three o'clock on Tuesday afternoon. She stepped out on the porch dressed in a shapeless black cotton knit dress, a red satin letterman jacket, tennies with pink socks, and a wide-brimmed yellow straw hat. "I've been ready to go for an hour."

"I came as soon as classes were out," Abbie explained. She took a deep breath to steady herself and asked, "Where would you like to go?" She hoped it wasn't another trip to the supermarket. She dreaded a return visit. Sunday's excursion had been little more than a loud series of complaints from one end of the large grocery store to the other. Couldn't Mrs. Merkel get along with anybody?

Mrs. Merkel turned to lock the front door behind her. "You know where the college is. There's a coffee shop right across the street from the main entrance to the college grounds. That's where I want to go."

Abbie relaxed. A coffee shop. That shouldn't be a problem—unless she ran into her father there. She didn't want to see him or talk to him. It was easier to pretend that he and his girlfriend didn't exist.

Except for tossing out a number of driving instructions, Mrs. Merkel didn't talk much as Abbie drove to the south end of Buckler and entered a wide U-shaped shopping strip across from the entrance to the college. At each side of the strip were two- and three-story office buildings. The first floor of the south office building contained a branch office of a banking chain, Unity National. Next to it was a large appliance store. The blocklong middle of the shopping strip consisted of a variety of shops, including two restaurants, a music store, a dry cleaner, a used-book store, and—at the corner, next to an upscale dress shop—a coffee shop.

"That's where I want to go—to that coffee shop," Mrs. Merkel ordered.

Abbie parked in front. At three-twenty in the afternoon there weren't many customers in the shop, so they had their choice of tables. Mrs. Merkel headed for a table at the window and plopped down, darting glances to each side as though defending a claim.

Her chair and the one opposite it were in direct sunlight. "The sun's coming right in on you," Abbie said. "Would you be more comfortable at one of the other tables?"

"No. I'm sitting here because I want to sit here," Mrs. Merkel answered. "I knew it would be sunny. That's why I wore this hat." She pulled a pen and her notebook from her handbag.

A man spoke up at the counter behind Abbie. "More coffee, Jamie girl?"

"You bet," a woman's voice answered.

"Gonna drive into Corpus Christi next week for the boat show?"

"That's the plan."

"With that egghead professor boyfriend of yours?"

Professor? Jamie? Abbie stiffened, gripping the edge of the Formica table. She turned her head slightly so that she could sneak a look at the waitress behind the counter. It was Jamie Lane. No doubt about it.

"I don't see a ring on your hand yet," the man teased.

"You will. Soon as we find one I like," Jamie said.

"Like a diamond big as a saucer?"

Jamie laughed. "How could a professor afford a diamond like that? No, I'd like an opal. I've always been partial to opals. I know a guy in the business. He's keeping an eye out for a nice opal ring."

Urgently Abbie leaned toward Mrs. Merkel. "I don't like this place," she said. "Let's find another coffee shop. Come on. Please. Let's go."

"I don't know why you've got ants in your pants," Mrs. Merkel snapped. "We aren't going anywhere. Sit down and behave yourself."

"Can't talk all day, Marvin. I've got some table customers," Abbie heard Jamie say.

Still holding tightly to the edge of the table, Abbie closed her eyes. She didn't open them until a voice just above and behind her asked pleasantly, "How about a cup of coffee, ladies?"

"I hate coffee. Never drink it. I'll have iced tea," Mrs. Merkel said. "With sugar and lemon. Make sure the glass is clean."

"And you?" Jamie asked as she turned her attention to Abbie. She took a step forward and bent, peering into Abbie's face. "Abbie? It is you, isn't it?"

Abbie sighed and leaned back. "Yes. I'm Abbie Thompson. I believe you know my parents—Sandra and Davis Thompson."

For the first time she took a good look at Jamie Lane. Up close she could see that Jamie wasn't as young as she had looked at a distance. Maybe the long, swinging hair had fooled her. Or Jamie's slender, almost boyish figure. But under the heavy makeup Abbie could see crow's-feet at the corners of Jamie's eyes and sag lines under her chin.

"I don't care to order anything, thank you," Abbie said coolly. She turned and glanced out the window, directing her attention to the wide arch across the street that spanned the entrance to Buckler College. Maybe her father was in the English department's building right now, teaching a late-afternoon class. Or maybe he was in his new apartment, waiting for Jamie's shift to be over.

"She'll have a Coke," Mrs. Merkel snapped. "And don't take forever with our order."

As Jamie left the table, Mrs. Merkel suddenly leaned toward Abbie. Lowering her voice, she asked, "What's the matter with you? You're supposed to order something and try to be unobtrusive, not identify yourself. We don't want people to pay much notice to us while we're working."

Abbie shot a look at Jamie, who had moved to the far end of the counter. "It was hard to even speak to that woman," she answered. "I hate her."

Mrs. Merkel squinted as she stared at Abbie. Finally she said, "She the one who hooked your father?"

When Abbie didn't answer, Mrs. Merkel said, "She probably doesn't like you any better'n you like her. When she brings your Coke, just shut up and drink it. We've got better things to do."

"Like what? Why are we sitting here?"

Mrs. Merkel didn't answer because Jamie returned with their drinks. Abbie was surprised to see Jamie's hands tremble a little as she carefully set the Coke glass on the table.

"Can I get you anything else?" Jamie asked Mrs. Merkel in her professionally cheerful voice.

"Just give us some privacy," Mrs. Merkel ordered. "Don't come back to the table to ask if everything's fine, because I can tell you right now that it is, and we don't want to be disturbed."

Without a word Jamie slapped their check on the table, turned, and left.

"You got any money to pay for that Coke you ordered or are you going to be a freeloader?" Mrs. Merkel asked Abbie.

Abbie met Mrs. Merkel's gaze. "I didn't order it. You did."

Mrs. Merkel put some money on top of the check. "Never mind. I'll put it down as a business expense. But this is the only time. After this, you pay for yourself. Now, keep your eyes open."

"For what?"

"Forget it. There she is. Confined to bed, is she?"

Abbie peered out the window, puzzled. All she saw was a late-model Lincoln pulling into a parking slot in front of the appliance store. If someone had gone into the store, she had missed seeing her.

Jamie laughed, and Abbie half turned, watching Jamie from the corners of her eyes. There were three more customers at the counter—all men. They chatted easily with Jamie, and it was obvious they liked her. Abbie had to admit that Jamie was a friendly person. She could hear Jamie asking one of the men about his children. She leaned forward on the counter, looking into his eyes, and seemed to be really interested in his answers.

Is that how it started with Dad? Abbie wondered.

Had Jamie begun by asking about his children? Had she acted terribly interested in everything he said?

"So that's where she's going—prissing right past us to M'Lady's like she owns the place," Mrs. Merkel said.

Mom was always interested. Didn't Dad pay attention? Abbie thought angrily. *Mom would always ask, "Did you have a good day, dear?"*

"So she got a look at me," Mrs. Merkel said, and chuckled. "Who cares? It just might give her something to lie awake nights wondering about."

Abbie remembered her mother often getting home from her job just minutes before Dad walked in the door. Kicking off her shoes, she'd check on dinner, or throw a load of washing in the machine, or sometimes greet Dad by saying, "Let's go to Luby's cafeteria for dinner. I'm totally beat." And somewhere in all the confusion, she'd manage to say, "Did you have a good day, dear?"

But she hadn't looked at Dad the way Jamie was looking at her customer. Mom had asked the question, but she hadn't always really, truly listened.

"That didn't take her long," Mrs. Merkel said. "Picking up a dress order, I guess."

It wasn't Mom's fault. She couldn't always listen, Abbie told herself. She felt the blood rising to her cheeks, and she touched them with the icy glass of Coke to cool them down. Sometimes Davy had been pestering Mom to listen to him. Sometimes Abbie knew she had done the same thing. *Oh, Dad,* she thought as tears burned behind her closed eyelids, *you weren't fair to Mom. You weren't fair to any of us.*

"Well, well. I guessed right. Figures. That makes sense. Close to the appliance store. Okay. We'll check things out."

Mrs. Merkel turned toward Abbie so suddenly, she startled her. "Are you still fooling around with your Coke? Drink it up. It's time to go."

Abbie took a long swallow.

"Were you paying attention to what I said?"

"Paying attention?" Guiltily Abbie looked at Mrs. Merkel.

"I told you," Mrs. Merkel said in a low voice, "that this is the biggest case anyone in Buckler's Bloodhounds will ever handle."

"What case?" Abbie asked in bewilderment.

"The one we're on now."

"If it's so big, shouldn't you tell what you know to Officer Martin?"

"And let her get the credit?"

Abbie sighed. Mrs. Merkel was so full of herself, it was hard to know if whatever she was talking about was real or not. "I think at least you ought to tell *someone* what you know, just to protect yourself."

"I'm telling *you.* Pay attention."

Abbie sighed. "I'm sorry. I haven't kept my mind on what you were saying. That waitress—"

"Get your mind off that waitress. She's your father's problem, not yours—at least, not right now."

92

"Look, if we could just get out of this place, I'd be happy," Abbie said.

Mrs. Merkel closed her notebook and dropped it into her handbag. But as she did, Abbie could see that more pages had been written on.

Awkwardly Mrs. Merkel pushed her chair away from the table and got to her feet. "That's what I was telling you. It's time to go," she said.

"Good." Abbie stood. "I wish we hadn't come here in the first place."

"Don't be stupid. Use your brains, girl. This has been one good place to watch from." She chuckled. "Now I've got two places—here and out my upstairs back window."

Abbie shook her head. "I don't ever want to come back here."

"We might not have to," Mrs. Merkel answered. "Not if what I suspect is true. But it's going to demand some deep investigating. How good are you with a computer?"

"I can use a computer. Why?" Abbie asked as she held the door open for Mrs. Merkel. Jamie didn't look up as they left the coffee shop, but Abbie suspected that she'd watch them through the large plate glass windows once the door was closed and they were out on the sidewalk.

"Do you know anything about hacking? Could you break into Unity National Bank's records?"

Abbie stopped and stared at Mrs. Merkel. "That's illegal. I can't do that."

"Can't or won't?"

"Both." Abbie caught up with Mrs. Merkel.

"Why would you want me to do a thing like that?"

"Because I can't think of any way the bank would let me see her records. I'd have to sneak in and get them."

"Whose records?"

Mrs. Merkel gripped Abbie's arm and yanked her along as she strode down the sidewalk.

"Where are we going?" Abbie asked.

"Where does it look like? The bank."

"Why? You said you did business with Gulf East Savings and Loan. This bank is Unity National, one of those big banking chains."

"Don't ask so many fool questions. I told you to go with me to the bank. That's all you need to know."

As they stepped inside the large bank lobby, the cold air-conditioning swept around Abbie like an arctic wave. She closed her eyes for an instant, enjoying the shivering sensation, then took a few steps in the direction of the row of tellers.

"Hssst! Over here," Mrs. Merkel whispered loudly. "Where do you think you're going?"

Surprised, Abbie turned in the direction of Mrs. Merkel's voice and saw her standing at one of the tall desks, pen in hand, bent over her notebook. Abbie walked to her side. "Oh. You *do* have an account here," she said.

"No, I don't," Mrs. Merkel answered crossly. "But I have to look like I do. You don't know the first thing about the way private investigators work, do you?

"Well, I—"

"You're no help at all. In fact, today you're *worse* than no help at all."

"Look, Mrs. Merkel, if you'd just tell me what you're doing and what you want me to do, I'd be glad to help you," Abbie said. "But I can't help if I don't know what's going on."

"I'm not about to tell you. This has all got to be kept secret."

"I'm good at keeping secrets. Trust me."

Mrs. Merkel glared at Abbie. "You're a criminal on probation, and a pretty stupid criminal at that. And you want me to trust you? Fat chance."

Abbie turned away, gripping her hands together so tightly that her fingers hurt. She faced a whole year of putting up with Mrs. Merkel and her meanness and rudeness. *How can I?* she wondered. Mrs. Merkel and Mrs. Wilhite—two nightmares come true.

As Abbie took deep breaths, trying to calm down, she reminded herself that she had to make this Friend to Friend thing work. She had made a huge mistake and must pay for it. She desperately wanted the arrest erased from her record. That meant she'd have to get along with Mrs. Merkel. She had no choice.

Abbie glanced around the bank. It was a prosperous branch with a large, ornamental lobby and many desks—not like the much smaller Gulf East Savings and Loan.

She turned toward Mrs. Merkel. "Those bank records you want—are they with this bank?"

Mrs. Merkel suddenly ducked her head, bending over the notebook. "Darn!" she said. "No more pages." But Abbie could see that she was grinning.

"Never mind what I said about hacking into records," Mrs. Merkel said. "I won't need them after all." She dropped the notebook into her handbag.

"Why not?"

"Hsst! Keep your head down! Look this way, and don't talk so loud."

"I'm sorry," Abbie said. She obediently leaned toward Mrs. Merkel, who was watching someone from the corner of her eye.

Mrs. Merkel suddenly stood upright. "Okay. It's safe now. Give her a few minutes, and we can go."

Abbie sighed. She was tired of Mrs. Merkel's games. "If you have some information the police should know about, why don't you call Officer Martin?"

Mrs. Merkel bristled. "Why don't *you* just mind your own business?"

"Please, Mrs. Merkel," Abbie said, "I don't know what you're doing. I just don't want you to get into any trouble."

"I can take care of myself," Mrs. Merkel snapped. She thought a moment, then said, "Except for driving. And you're my driver. So why are we hanging around here? Let's get going."

Again gripping Abbie's arm, Mrs. Merkel left the sidewalk to cut across the parking lot. They had begun to cross a driving lane when Abbie suddenly realized that a gray sedan was coming down the lane much faster than it should.

"Get back," she said, tugging at Mrs. Merkel.

Mrs. Merkel resisted, staring at the car. "Stop that! Leave me alone! I can't read the license plate," she complained.

The car wasn't slowing. It seemed to be speeding up.

"Look out!" Abbie shouted. "He's going to hit you!"

—————————————————————————

bbie flung her arm around Mrs. Merkel's neck and dragged her between two parked cars. As they slammed against the trunk of one car and bounced off the side door of the other, Abbie struggled to regain her balance.

Indignantly Mrs. Merkel jerked away. She stood erect, dusting off her clothes. "What do you think you're doing?" she angrily demanded.

"Saving your life," Abbie told her. "That car was headed right for us. Didn't you see how fast he was traveling? The driver didn't even slow down."

"I was trying to get a good look at the license plate, and you didn't let me," Mrs. Merkel complained. "I'm sure that gray car belongs to the crook who was stealing cell phone numbers."

"It couldn't be. He was arrested. That was just another parking lot speeder."

"It was the crook," Mrs. Merkel insisted.

"Did you see him driving the car?"

"Of course not. How could I see, with you pushing me around like that?" Furious, Mrs. Merkel gave Abbie a shove. "Take me home," she insisted. "I'm going to call Officer Martin and find out if that stupid perp is back on the street."

Mrs. Merkel plopped herself on the front seat of the car, breaking her angry silence on the ride home only to issue her usual driving instructions and warnings.

Abbie parked the car and followed Mrs. Merkel inside, waiting while she jabbed the buttons on her phone and demanded to speak to Officer Amanda Martin.

After a very short conversation, during which Mrs. Merkel's anger continued to grow, she slammed down the receiver and whirled toward Abbie. "Would you believe he made bail? Those roofers, too!"

"They're free?" Abbie began to feel fear creep like a cold chill up her backbone.

"That's what I said."

Abbie began to worry. What if that hadn't been just a reckless driver in the parking lot? "When you told Officer Martin about the car that almost hit us, what did she say?"

"She said she didn't see why it would be the

guy stealing cell phone numbers. She was sure he'd stay out of sight and keep clean until he has to go to court. But she did offer to keep an eye on my house. That probably means a squad car will drive past once or twice a day. Ha! A fat lot of good that's going to do!"

"Mrs. Merkel, you challenged those men and had them arrested. They're angry with you. I don't think you should be alone," Abbie said. "Could your nephew come and stay with you for a while?"

"Charlie? I can't see that greedy bum doing me any favors, especially when I refused to do any more for him."

"Then maybe one of your friends?" In the pause that followed Abbie suggested, "What about Effie Glebe?"

"No! Not Effie. After that squabble about . . . Well, never mind. Effie and I aren't speaking—no loss to me."

Sure that none of the members in the former book club felt friendly enough to volunteer, Abbie took a deep breath, hoping her mother would understand what she was doing. "For your own safety," Abbie asked, "why don't you stay with my family—at least for a few days?"

Mrs. Merkel scowled. "Not on your life. No little two-bit perp is going to drive me out of my own house!"

"It would be only for a short while. Just until those men are tried and convicted."

"Who says they will be? If the police can't even hang on to them . . ." A strange, almost wistful look came over her face, and she said, "Maybe they should get together—all the stupid people who'd like me out of the way."

"All what people? Who are they?"

Mrs. Merkel gripped the back of a chair, snarling, "Don't ask personal questions. I wasn't talking to you. I was talking to myself. I'm not about to bare my private life to a silly twit like you."

Abbie forced back the answer she'd like to give Mrs. Merkel. This was no time for hurt feelings. She had to get back to the subject of Mrs. Merkel's safety. "Don't blame the police for the crooks being out on bail," she said. "If the judge sets a low enough bail and the crooks can make it, the police can't do a thing about it. Their job was only to catch the crooks, and—"

"You're wrong. My job was to catch them."

Abbie sighed and sat in the nearest chair. "Regardless, I don't want them to come here looking for you," she said.

"After what I did to them, they wouldn't dare tangle with me," Mrs. Merkel bragged. But she suddenly sat down and sagged in the lumpy plush chair. She looked very old and very tired.

"Would you like a glass of water?" Abbie asked.

"No," Mrs. Merkel said. "Be quiet. I'm trying to think."

Abbie sat very still, feeling the silence of the old house creep around her. From overhead came a creaking sound. Was someone on the roof? Abbie wrapped her arms around herself, shivering.

All at once the faint tinkle of the music from an ice cream truck down the street broke the spell. Somewhere outside a child laughed, and the brakes of a heavy truck down on Main Street squealed and whined to a stop. With the sounds of the world back to normal, Abbie began to relax. Why had she let herself worry so much? Mrs. Merkel certainly was able to take care of herself, and with the police alerted, she wouldn't be in danger.

The intrusion from outside seemed to help Mrs. Merkel pull herself together too. She sat up and snapped open her handbag. Slowly she removed her green notebook. Without a word she stood and went to her desk. After rummaging through two of the drawers, she pulled out a small manila envelope, dropped the notebook inside, and sealed the flap.

Next she walked to Abbie and handed the envelope to her. "Just in case anybody comes poking around here while I'm gone, I'd better put this in a safe place," she said. "They won't think of looking in your house, so you find a good hiding place and keep this away from prying eyes."

"Don't you want to keep it in your handbag so it's there when you need to make notes?"

Mrs. Merkel rolled her eyes. "Use your brains, girl. Why would I carry around a notebook that's all used up with no more pages to write on? I've got to get me a new one, but this one has important notes in it, so I need to keep it safe."

As she stood, Abbie took the envelope. "I'll keep it safe," she said.

Mrs. Merkel smirked. "Don't bother snooping, trying to read it. You saw that I sealed the envelope. I'll know if you tried to open it."

"I won't read it. Trust me," Abbie began. She shook her head. "Never mind. I remember what you said. You don't trust anybody."

"Why should I?" Mrs. Merkel said. It wasn't a real question, so Abbie didn't try to answer.

"I should get home and start dinner," she told Mrs. Merkel. "Are you sure you'll be all right without me?"

"Better than I am with you. Be here on time tomorrow."

"Tomorrow? You don't expect me to come every day, I hope. Mrs. Wilhite told us only two or three days a week."

Mrs. Merkel leaned close. Her eyes were slits, glittering with malice. "That rule's for the other girls," she said. "You're a special case. You wouldn't want me to report to Mrs. Wilhite that you were uncooperative and I'd had to fire you, would you?"

"No," Abbie answered slowly as she fought to control her feelings. "I'll be here tomorrow."

She walked out to her car flushed with anger. *I don't want to see her tomorrow. Or the next day. Or ever!*

As she turned the key in the ignition, Abbie groaned aloud. *One whole year of Mrs. Merkel,* she thought with dread. *How in the world will I be able to stand it?*

The telephone was ringing as Abbie entered the kitchen. She sprinted to answer the ring, grabbed the receiver, and said, "Hello?"

"Hi," Gigi answered. "I met my Friend today—Mrs. Gertrude Armistead. She's darling. She's typecast right out of a movie. She's just what a great-grandmother ought to be." Gigi laughed with delight. "And guess what—she's not a hundred. She's only eighty-nine. But she wears a perfume that smells like marshmallows and she loves to eat chocolate."

Abbie laughed too. "Lucky you," she said, surprised to hear a twinge of envy in her own voice. Trying to make up for it before Gigi noticed, she quickly said, "What did you do? Did you drive her somewhere?"

"No. Mrs. Armistead loves to play Chinese checkers and usually has no one to play with, so we drank iced tea with mint and played Chinese checkers."

Abbie smiled. "You and I played Chinese checkers for years when we were kids. Remember? Dad used to join us sometimes and . . ." She broke off. "So who won? You or Mrs. Armistead?"

"She did," Gigi said. "I thought maybe I'd have to let her win, like you do when you're playing with little kids, but she's a lot better player than I am. She told me I needed practice to keep up with her."

"I'm glad you got somebody nice," Abbie said.

"I could count on it that whomever I got would be better than your Mrs. Merkel," Gigi said. "How did it go today? Is she still hunting for criminals?"

"She still thinks she's a private eye," Abbie said. "We went to a coffee shop where she could spy on someone out the window."

Gigi laughed. "Who did she spy on?" she asked.

Abbie searched her mind for an answer, surprised that she could come up with nothing. "I don't know," she said.

"What do you mean, you don't know? You were with her, weren't you?"

Abbie sighed. "Yes, but I was kind of distracted. Dad's . . . uh . . . that . . . Jamie Lane was our waitress."

"Uh-oh."

"I know. I asked Mrs. Merkel if we could leave and go somewhere else, but she said no. She didn't care that being so close to that woman was really bothering me."

"I'm sorry you had a rough time," Gigi said.

Abbie thought about telling Gigi the rest of it—the car that almost ran them down, the crooks out of jail on bail, and the notebook filled with Mrs. Merkel's secret notes. But at the moment she couldn't talk about all that. Her only hope was to change the subject. "Want to go to a movie Sunday afternoon?" she asked.

"Sure," Gigi said, and she began telling Abbie

in detail about an Internet review of a new film they both wanted to see.

Abbie could hear Davy clumping down the stairs. In a moment he appeared in the kitchen doorway. He waved the thin, three-hole notebook over his head. "Come on," he said in an exaggerated stage whisper. "You've got to tell me everything that happened before Mom gets home and it's too late."

Whatever Gigi was talking about at that moment was drowned out. Or maybe Abbie hadn't been paying attention in the first place. She couldn't seem to get her mind off Mrs. Merkel. She nodded at Davy and said to Gigi, "Davy's home. I've got to go."

"Okay," Gigi said cheerfully. "See you tomorrow."

"Right. Tomorrow." Abbie hung up and followed Davy to the kitchen table, where he opened his notebook and took out a ballpoint pen.

"Start talking," he said importantly. "Tell me everything that happened."

Abbie wanted to run upstairs, fling herself on the bed, and never come out of her room again. But she reminded herself she was doing this to help Davy. Involving him had already made a difference. He was talking to her. And he had stopped acting so angry.

"Mrs. Merkel told me to drive her to that coffee shop across the street from the entrance to the college," she said. For an instant she expected him to react, but he just concentrated on what he was writing, seemingly unconcerned. *There's no reason he should know that Jamie Lane is a waitress or where she works*, Abbie thought, so she continued, leaving Jamie out of it.

"We had to sit at a window table so that Mrs. Merkel could spy on someone."

"Who?"

"I—I don't know. I wasn't paying attention."

At this Davy sat up and stared at Abbie. "You were with her. You were sitting right there, weren't you? How could you not be paying attention?"

"I guess I was distracted."

"Abbie, this isn't going to work if you don't notice what's going on. Now, think about it. What did she say? What did you see? I've got to write down everything I can about what happened."

Abbie nodded. "Mrs. Merkel said she was working on the biggest case Buckler's Bloodhounds would ever handle."

"Good. Good. What's the case about?"

"She wouldn't tell me. She keeps saying if she tells me things I'll probably blab them."

"You wouldn't do that. She's weird," Davy said, but he kept writing.

Abbie felt a comforting warmth sweep through her. Davy was a good kid. No matter how much of a pest he could sometimes be, he was her brother and she loved him. "Okay, let's see," she said, searching her brain for every scrap of information she could remember. "The person she was spying on was a woman who went into that expensive dress shop next to the coffee shop."

Davy looked up, blank for a moment.

"It's a women's dress shop, and everything there costs too much money. But this woman did buy something."

"How do you know?"

Surprised that Mrs. Merkel's words had popped into her mind, Abbie answered, "Mrs. Merkel said something about the woman picking up an order."

"Was the woman already in the dress shop when you got to the coffee shop?" Davy asked.

"No . . . no. She arrived after we were seated at the table."

"How did she get there?"

A sudden memory made Abbie jump. "I think she was driving a white Lincoln."

"Town Car?"

"I don't know."

"Big?"

"Yes."

"Town Car," Davy said as he wrote. "Tell me more."

Abbie found herself telling Davy about following Mrs. Merkel to the bank.

"Was the woman there?"

"I don't know. I didn't see her."

"Didn't you ask Mrs. Merkel why you were in the bank?"

"Yes, but she told me to mind my own business."

"She is really, truly weird," Davy said. "If I ever need to hire a private eye, it won't be her."

They continued until Davy had all his questions answered and Abbie couldn't remember another thing about the mystery woman. Davy stood, clutching the closed notebook to his chest. "Mom should be home pretty soon," he said. "I'll put this back in its hiding place."

Abbie thought about the notebook Mrs. Merkel had given to her to hide. She hadn't mentioned the notebook to Davy, and she wasn't about to. She knew where she'd hide it—between her mattress and box spring. As hiding places go, it wouldn't be an imaginative place, but that didn't matter. Hiding the notebook was just something to do to please Mrs. Merkel. No one would come looking for it. No one would care.

Taking the envelope from her backpack, Abbie hid it just where she had planned.

"Now what?" she asked her reflection in the mirror over her chest of drawers, but the reflection stared back with a blank, almost questioning look. If there were any answers, Abbie certainly didn't have them.

CHAPTER ELEVEN

Mrs. Thompson arrived home late for dinner. Abbie had made a baked chicken dish, and around the edges of the Pyrex pan the Italian sauce had dried in ragged black curls. "I'm sorry," Abbie said, but her mother took a bite and tried to look blissful as she chewed it.

"I like it crispy," she said. "It's delicious."

Davy ate quietly, but when Mrs. Thompson asked him what he'd done in school he opened up and told her about the science project he was working on with P.J.

Abbie could see the surprise in her mother's eyes and her eagerness to soak up every one of Davy's words.

After he'd asked to be excused and had bolted

110

from the kitchen, Mrs. Thompson turned to Abbie. "Davy's coming around," she murmured in delight. "I've been pricing therapists, trying to find the right one—one who'd understand, one I could afford. But maybe things will work out without therapy. Tonight he was so much like he used to be." She leaned back in her chair and sighed. "He didn't seem angry with me."

"Mom, Davy's not angry at you," Abbie said. She reached over to place a hand over her mother's. "He's angry at what he doesn't understand. His whole world has changed, and he doesn't know why."

Mrs. Thompson's hand turned so that her fingers could curl around Abbie's. She gave Abbie's hand a squeeze and looked into her eyes. "Is it that way with you, too? Are you angry because you can't understand what has happened?"

"No," Abbie said. "I do understand what happened. It's simple. Dad doesn't care about us. He only cares about himself. He wants to believe that he's still young and good-looking, and he found a woman who'll help with his make-believe."

"A very young woman."

"She's not so young," Abbie blurted out. "She's got crow's-feet and wrinkles under her chin, and her neck's beginning to sag."

As her mother instinctively touched her own chin with the tips of her fingers, Abbie added, "You should see her up close. She wears too much makeup, probably trying to cover a lot of flaws."

Mrs. Thompson studied Abbie closely. "How do you know all this?" she suddenly asked.

"She works as a waitress in the coffee shop across the street from the entrance to the college," Abbie said. "Mrs. Merkel and I . . . we stopped there for soft drinks."

"So that's where he met her," Mrs. Thompson said softly. She thought for a moment, then asked, "What were you doing out by the college?"

Abbie shrugged. "Mom," she said, "Mrs. Merkel calls me her driver. She says that's all I'm good for. I just take her wherever she wants to go."

But Abbie could see the wheels still going around in her mother's mind. "Why that particular coffee shop?" Mrs. Thompson asked.

Abbie wasn't sure if the question was meant for her or if her mother was asking herself, but she said, "Mrs. Merkel went to that big bank in the same shopping center. She wanted to stop for some iced tea first."

"Oh," Mrs. Thompson said. She seemed satisfied. "How are things working out with your Mrs. Merkel?"

Why does everyone call her my *Mrs. Merkel?* Abbie wanted to shout. For just an instant she wondered if she should confide in her mother about Mrs. Merkel's activities. But she knew the answer was a strong no. Her mother would be alarmed, she would complain to Mrs. Wilhite, Abbie would be pulled from the Friend to Friend program, and who knew what the judge would decide to do to her?

"Why are you shaking your head?" Mrs. Thompson asked.

"Was I?" Abbie asked, startled. "Oh, I was just thinking about Mrs. Merkel. She gets kind of crabby at times." Abbie looked at her mother, desperate for an answer. "Does everybody get like that when they're old? I don't want you to get crabby, Mom, and I don't want to be crabby either."

Mrs. Thompson laughed. "I once read that when you get old you just become more of what you already are. If you've always had a sense of humor and liked people, you just become nicer. If you've always been a grouch, you probably get to be more of a grouch."

Abbie laughed. "I think Mrs. Merkel was born a grouch," she said.

Mrs. Thompson stood. Before she picked up her plate and utensils to take them to the sink, she bent to kiss Abbie's forehead. "I'm doubly proud of you for being able to get along with her," she said. "When will you go back to visit her? Thursday? Saturday?"

"Tomorrow. Wednesday," Abbie said, and sighed. "She told me it was very important."

Frowning, Mrs. Thompson said, "You don't have to visit her every day. I read the material you were sent. It said two or three times a week."

"I know, Mom," Abbie said. "But she insisted.

So just tomorrow I'll need the car again. Okay? I'll try to work things out with her."

Mrs. Thompson nodded as she opened the dishwasher. "Okay, honey. After I get these dishes in here, I'm going upstairs to take a long bath. I'm tired, right down to my toes."

Abbie began to carry the rest of the dishes to the sink. "Take your bath now, Mom. I'll do the dishes," she said.

Gratefully Abbie's mother kissed her again and left the kitchen. Abbie could hear her in the den, cautioning Davy to do his homework before watching television. But the TV's volume grew even higher after Mrs. Thompson's footsteps sounded on the stairs.

Abbie had just finished loading the dishwasher and was drying her hands on the kitchen towel when someone knocked on the outside door to the kitchen. Startled, she looked out the window, into the shadows of the deepening twilight, and saw her father standing on the kitchen steps.

She began to back away, but he had glimpsed her and called out, "It's just me, Abbie. You don't need to be alarmed."

A key turned in the lock, and the door opened. "I didn't want to frighten you by just walking in," he said. "That's why I knocked."

Abbie leaned against the kitchen counter for support. *Mom should have changed the locks*, she thought. *Did she think Dad would be sorry and come back? Did she hope everything would be the same again?* "Mom's not here," she told her father. "She went upstairs."

"I didn't come here to talk to your mother," Dr. Thompson said. "I came to talk to you, honey."

"I'm not here either," Abbie told him. "Remember? I'm nobody. I'm nothing."

He frowned, looking puzzled. "Don't play games," he said. "Let's get to the point. You were in a situation today in which you could have been pleasant and polite to Jamie. Instead you were rude. She was distressed."

"She tattled to you?"

"I don't like your choice of words, Abbie. She simply confided her unhappiness."

Abbie gripped the edge of the counter. "I wasn't intentionally rude to her. I was . . . well, you could say, *distressed*, myself, when she came to our table. I didn't know she worked there."

Dr. Thompson looked stern. "Did you say hello pleasantly, as you've been trained to do?"

Taking a deep breath, fighting down her resentment, Abbie said, "Now *you've* used the wrong word, Dad. *Taught* is what you should have said, not *trained*. Trained is what you do with pet poodles."

He flushed but continued. "Did you call Jamie by name—Ms. Lane—and introduce her to your guest?"

"Dad—"

"Or did you encourage your guest to be rude to Jamie too?"

Abbie pushed herself away from the support of the counter, taking a step toward her father. "The woman I was with was not my guest. She

115

was assigned to me in that Friend to Friend thing I'm doing while I'm on probation. Mrs. Merkel has a mean disposition, and she's rude to everyone, including me."

"Don't exaggerate, Abbie. It doesn't help your case."

"Case? Am I on trial? Did you come to talk to me or just to lecture me? Don't you want to hear my side of what happened?"

"No, I don't," Dr. Thompson said. "It's important to me that Jamie is happy and feels accepted."

Abbie opened her mouth to speak, but her father interrupted. Reaching for her hand, he said, "Abbie, honey, this is all very difficult for me."

Abbie jerked away. "For *you*, Dad? It doesn't have to be."

"You don't understand."

"No, I don't."

"If you'd just try . . ." He stopped speaking, frowning as he thought. Finally he raised his head, looking at Abbie with a sorrowful expression. "Abbie, I hope you understand that I will not tolerate your causing Jamie to be unhappy. You will not behave rudely to her in the future."

"But I didn't. That is, I won't. I—"

"There is no reason for you to go to that particular coffee shop again. I forbid it."

"You can't! Dad, I have to take Mrs. Merkel wherever she wants me to go, and she told me we were going back to that coffee shop."

"That's an easy problem to remedy. You can encourage her to go somewhere else."

"You don't understand. She has . . . well, a certain project in mind."

"It doesn't matter."

"Yes, it does. If I don't do what Mrs. Merkel wants, she can cause trouble for me."

Dr. Thompson sighed. "The trouble you find yourself in is trouble you have caused for yourself. I've given you an order. You are absolutely not to go inside that coffee shop again, and when you meet Jamie in the future—under happier circumstances, I hope—you are to be polite and pleasant. I'd like to plan sailing dates with you and Davy and Jamie in the near future. Theater productions at the college, weekends in Corpus Christi—there are endless possibilities for family activities. Do you understand why it's important for you to have a good relationship with Jamie?"

"You are not acting like my father, so why should I do what you want me to do?" Angry and frustrated, Abbie burst into tears.

When she was finally able to control her sobs and was wiping her eyes on the kitchen towel, she saw that her father had left.

"Abbie?" Mrs. Thompson spoke from the door that led into the den. "Honey? Were you crying?"

Abbie nodded. She moved into her mother's open arms and rested her damp cheek against her mother's, inhaling the fragrances of bath oil and lotion, hungry for comfort.

Finally her mother stepped back and searched Abby's face. "What happened?" she asked. "What made you cry?"

Abbie gently shook her head. She couldn't handle all the problems that had been dumped on her. Mrs. Merkel . . . Jamie Lane . . . her father.

And she couldn't tell her mother everything that had happened. She couldn't even tell her that her father had just been there. Her mother would be angry and hurt, maybe even frightened. She had enough to worry her. Testing, Abbie found she could speak without setting off a fresh batch of tears.

"I won't need the car tomorrow Mom," she said. "I'm not going to visit Mrs. Merkel after all. I've got homework and a long-term project in English."

"You're right to limit your visits," Mrs. Thompson agreed. "The Friend to Friend people don't expect you to go every day."

At the moment Abbie didn't care what Mrs. Merkel might do to her. She didn't care if she ever saw Mrs. Merkel again. She felt the way she had when she was a little girl. Inside her mother's arms nothing could harm her, nothing could frighten her. "Hold me tight, Mom," Abbie said, and stepped into another of her mother's hugs.

CHAPTER TWELVE

At the school gate the next morning, Nick Campos met Abbie with a wide grin.

Abbie's heart gave a lurch. She liked Nick. Probably if her life hadn't changed so drastically, she'd be thrilled to date him. But now she didn't know anything for sure. She definitely didn't want to get hurt.

"After school let's walk down to the Dairy Queen and get a cone," Nick suggested. "I've got a question for you, and you can answer me then. Okay?"

Abbie smiled. "Okay," she said. "I'll meet you at my locker."

Twice during the day Abbie thought about Mrs. Merkel. Once she almost telephoned to let her know she wasn't coming, but she stopped herself in time.

She doesn't own me, Abbie told herself, and walked away from the telephone. If she did call, Mrs. Merkel would either yell at her and try to make her feel guilty, or she'd threaten Abbie, forcing her into coming. *No!* Abbie told herself. *My life is my own, and I'm going to have ice cream with Nick if I feel like it.*

By the time she and Nick were seated in a booth at the nearby Dairy Queen, Abbie had pushed any guilt away completely and defiantly. But her feelings about being with Nick were muddled. She knew she could like him a lot. But how could she trust what any guy said?

Her mother had trusted her father. She had trusted him enough to fall deeply in love, and she'd married him with trust. Then her father had thrown that trust away. He wasn't alone. Every women's magazine ran articles aimed at divorced moms. Did all guys walk away from their families the way Dad had?

The few dates Abbie had had so far weren't what she'd call wonderful. Manning's attack of hay fever at a barn dance, Jimmy's popcorn-greasy hand holding hers at a movie . . . she recalled a series of sweaty palms, damp kisses, bruised male egos. Wouldn't it be better to forget the whole dating thing and escape a lot of hurt?

But while they ate their cones, Nick told Abbie funny stories and made her laugh. And Nick asked her to the junior prom. He complained about having two left feet and stumbling around on a dance floor until Abbie found herself promising to teach him to dance.

She was totally flattered that Nick had invited her to the prom, but she didn't know what to say. *Better not,* she told herself, *but . . .*

She suddenly glanced up at the round clock on the wall and gave a start. "It's almost five!" she said.

Nick grinned. "Time flies—"

"I know," Abbie said. "When you're having fun."

"Were you?"

"Yes, I was," she answered, and smiled at him.

"When do I get my first dance lesson?" he asked.

Abbie hesitated. Now came the reality, the time spent together, the questions without answers. "I don't know yet," she said quickly as she slid from the booth. "I'll let you know. Okay?"

As she walked home, thoughts of Mrs. Merkel swept into Abbie's mind like a swarm of bees. She tried to brush them away. It was Nick she wanted to think about. Did she want to go to the junior prom with him? She hadn't given him an answer. Wouldn't it be easier to just walk away, close her mind, shut him out, protect herself from the hurt he might cause her?

But in her mind Mrs. Merkel's face kept popping up, erasing Nick's big smile. Mrs. Merkel wasn't wearing her usual cross expression. She looked as she had the day before when she had dropped into a chair, tired and old, and probably a little frightened, in spite of what she had said. *I should have gone to visit her as she asked me to,* Abbie thought as she unlocked the back door and entered the kitchen. *Maybe I still can.*

No. Mom had the car. There was no way Abbie could get to Mrs. Merkel's house without a car. Thick as syrup, guilt began to spread through Abbie's body, making her feel a little sick.

I could go after dinner, she told herself. *That's what I'll do. I'll take whatever scolding Mrs. Merkel gives me, but at least she'll realize she can't threaten me into going to see her every single day.*

As she dropped her book-laden backpack on the table, Davy ran into the room, notebook in hand. He shoved aside her pack, making space on the table, and opened his notebook. "Okay," he said. "Start talking. What did Mrs. Merkel do today?"

"I didn't go today," Abbie told him.

"Why not?"

"Because . . . I had other things to do." Quickly she defended herself. "I'm not even supposed to go every day."

Davy looked so disappointed that Abbie said, "I'm going after dinner, after Mom gets back with the car." She tried to ease the situation by adding, "I'll try to remember every single thing she says and does and tell you when I get home. Okay?"

Davy stood and shrugged. "Okay, I guess. But you won't go out spying on crooks at night, will you?"

I hope not! Abbie thought, but she said, "Who knows what Mrs. Merkel will want to do?"

122

"Yeah," Davy said. He immediately perked up. He jumped from his chair and snatched the notebook. "Gotta hide this," he said, and ran from the room.

Mrs. Thompson came home early, carrying a bag filled with takeout cartons from a Chinese restaurant near her office. "You need a break," she said to Abbie. "I got shrimp lo mein, beef and snow peas, and that garlic pork you like." She sniffed inside the bag and sighed with pleasure.

As the three of them gathered around the table, sharing the food, Abbie wondered if the others remembered what it was like when Dad was still with them and they indulged in a feast of Chinese food. Dad had always loved sweet-and-sour chicken and put dibs on seconds. Dad had— She pushed away thoughts of her father. He no longer had a part in their feasts. He didn't belong with them anymore. Not because they wanted it that way, but because *he* did.

"Mom," Davy said indistinctly, his mouth full, "Abbie needs to use your car tonight."

Mrs. Thompson looked from Davy to Abbie and back to Davy. "What's up?" she asked.

"Nothing," Davy said, trying to cover his eagerness. "Abbie didn't go to see Mrs. Merkel today, so she needs to go tonight."

Mrs. Thompson smiled at Abbie reassuringly. "She didn't need to go this afternoon, and she certainly doesn't have to go tonight."

"But—" Davy looked at Abbie.

"Mom, I did promise her I would come," Abbie said. "I'm just going to drop by and ask how she is. That's all."

"You know you don't have to," Mrs. Thompson reminded her.

"I know. But I want to. Is it okay if I use the car?"

"Of course," Mrs. Thompson said, "but only if you really want to visit her."

"I do, Mom," Abbie answered.

"Davy, it's your turn to clean the kitchen," Mrs. Thompson said.

"Aw . . ." While Davy tried to think up a logical reason why he should be excused, Abbie borrowed her mother's car keys and drove to Mrs. Merkel's house.

Darnell Street was bathed in the pink glow of sunset reflected off piles of cottony clouds. Abbie took a long breath, bracing herself for whatever was going to happen. She stepped into the shadow of Mrs. Merkel's porch and rang the doorbell.

She waited a few minutes, listening for footsteps or Mrs. Merkel's voice, but no sound came from inside the house. Abbie rang the bell again, then realized there were no lights inside the house. Had Mrs. Merkel gone out for a walk? She had said she liked to walk.

A strange chill began at the nape of Abbie's neck, trickling through her back and arms. *Nothing's wrong*, she told herself. *The police said they'd drive by her house, and Mrs. Merkel wouldn't open the door to just anybody. She may be upstairs. That's it. She didn't hear the doorbell.*

Abbie pounded loudly on the door, wincing because the loud hammering jarred the quiet neighborhood.

No one answered. The house remained completely silent.

Abbie stepped to the side of the porch, leaning toward the nearest window. She cupped her hands and pressed her face and nose against the glass, trying to peer through the lace curtains into the room.

At first it was impossible to see through the gloom, but one at a time shapes began making themselves known, turning into a sofa . . . chairs . . . a desk . . . a coffee table . . .

As Abbie squinted, straining to examine the room, two white objects began to stand out. On the floor, sticking out from behind the coffee table, were a pair of tennis shoes. Inside the shoes were dark socks, and inside the socks . . .

Abbie shrieked and jumped back, nearly falling over the porch railing. She ran to the door, tugging, hammering, struggling to open it, but it was locked.

"What's the matter?" someone called.

Abbie leaped back and turned to see a woman standing on her porch next door. "It's Mrs. Merkel!" Abbie shouted. "She's lying on the floor! Call an ambulance! Call the police!"

The woman put her hands to her face. Her eyes widened with horror. "Is she dead?" she whispered.

"I don't know," Abbie cried out. "Please! Call 911! Hurry! If she's alive she needs help!"

The woman disappeared inside her house, scuttling like a frightened rabbit. Abbie tried the door again, although she knew it wouldn't do any good. As she ran down the steps, heading for the back of the house, she stopped to tug something from the sole of her right shoe. It was a wad of sticky tape. She didn't stop to wonder what it was doing on Mrs. Merkel's steps. She was in too big a hurry. She leaped over broken stepping-stones and jumped to the top of the back steps to shake and wiggle the knob on the door, but it held fast.

Stumbling and tripping as she turned and raced back to the front of the house, Abbie scratched her hands and knees on the broken stones. She scrambled to her feet, ran forward and fell again. She cried out in frustration as she tried her best to hurry. She had to get into the house! She must get help! Mrs. Merkel needed her!

As she rounded the corner of the house, she heard sirens in the distance. The neighbor she had called on for help stood at the edge of the lawn, a little closer but still at a safe distance, as though something in Mrs. Merkel's house could harm her if she drew close enough.

A half dozen other neighbors stood nearby on the sidewalk, their faces eager for news.

"What happened?"

"Is something wrong with Mrs. Merkel?"

"She isn't dead, is she?"

Abbie winced. She didn't try to answer. She

ran toward the curb as both an ambulance and a police car drove onto Darnell Street.

She headed for the ambulance first, shouting to the paramedics who hopped out, "She's lying on the floor! You can see her through the window!"

Motioning to the police officers who walked toward her, she said, "The front door's locked. So is the back door."

As one officer trotted up to the porch to join the paramedics, the other officer pushed back his hat and pulled out a notebook. "Are you the one who called us?"

"No," Abbie said, and pointed at the neighbor.

"Ma'am?" the officer asked, but the woman backed away. "I don't know anything about this," she said. She pointed in turn at Abbie. "She's the one who saw her. She told me to call."

Abbie heard the thud of the door being forced open. She turned and took a few steps toward the porch, but the officer said, "Wait a minute, young lady. Let them do their job without interference. You stay here. I need to ask you some questions."

"But I want to know—"

"They'll tell you soon enough. Now, first . . . what's your name and address?"

Impatiently shifting her weight from foot to foot, Abbie answered his questions, watching while he carefully filled out some kind of form he had in his notebook. She described her connection to Mrs. Merkel through the Friend to Friend program, which explained why she had come to visit.

Finally Abbie could stand no more questioning. "Could we find out how she is now?" she asked. "Please?"

"Sure," the officer said as he pocketed his notebook. "My partner probably has more questions for you."

Abbie was puzzled. "More questions? Like what?"

"Like do you know the name and address of her nearest relatives? Things like that."

Although the officer's strides were long, Abbie beat him to the front door. She stood on the porch, watching the paramedics, who knelt on the floor working on Mrs. Merkel. That meant she was alive. Abbie breathed a sigh of relief. The room was a mess. Things had been thrown out of the bookcases and the desk, as though someone had been looking for something.

As the other police officer realized Abbie was there and turned to look at her, she quickly asked, "Is Mrs. Merkel sick? Did she have a heart attack?"

The second officer looked questioningly at the first. He nodded and said, "You can tell her."

The officer looked away and dropped his voice. "She was attacked," he said. "Someone bashed her in the head. She's still alive, but the medics say she's barely hanging on."

"What was she hit with?"

"We couldn't find a weapon." He looked directly into Abbie's eyes as he asked, "Do you have any idea who could have attacked her?"

"No," Abbie quickly answered. Then, "Yes," she added. "I mean I can think of a few people who could have done it."

His eyebrows rose in surprise. "A few? You mean a gang?"

"Not a gang," Abbie said. She told him about Officer Amanda Martin's Buckler's Bloodhounds, the fake roofers who had threatened revenge, and the guy who stole cell phone numbers and had come at Mrs. Merkel in his speeding car.

As she finished her answer, the officer nearest the door said, "A TV crew just arrived." He looked down at Abbie. "I don't think you want to talk to them. Let's take you out the back door. You want a ride home?"

"No, thanks," Abbie said. "I drove my mom's car. It's right out in front."

The officer took her arm and led her through a small dining room into the kitchen. Abbie noticed that the kitchen was as tidy as the living room had been, with just one exception—a half-filled cup of coffee and a jar of instant coffee granules lay on the counter next to the stove.

Whoever had come had interrupted Mrs. Merkel as she was drinking a cup of coffee. She had left the kitchen to answer the front door and . . . Abbie shuddered.

"I don't want to go home," she said to the police officer. "I want to go with Mrs. Merkel to the hospital."

"Since you're not a relative, they may not let

you ride in the ambulance with her," he said, "but they'll take her to Mercy Hospital. You can drive over there and they'll probably let you see her."

"Thanks," Abbie said. "I'll do that."

"If you and the old lady are good friends . . . well, the news you get from Emergency might be kind of hard to take. Why don't you go home and get your mom and dad to go to the hospital with you?"

Abbie just nodded.

"When you go outside, watch out for the media. Somebody from the *Buckler Bee* should also be showing up about now. Don't talk to anyone. Go straight to your car and leave."

Abbie gave him a wave, ran down the back steps, and carefully picked her way across the broken stepping-stones until she reached Mrs. Merkel's front yard.

Darkness had settled in. The streetlights down the block spilled small pools of brightness, while the lights on the squad car and ambulance flickered like blue-and-red fireflies. It was easy for Abbie to mingle with the neighbors who were clustered in chattering clumps. She slipped from one group to the next until she was inside her car.

For just an instant she collapsed, emotionally exhausted, and rested her head on the steering wheel. If she had come after school, when she had promised, she would have been there to support Mrs. Merkel. Maybe the person who had

130

hurt Mrs. Merkel would have backed off if she hadn't been alone.

"It's my fault," Abbie murmured. She sat up, gripping the steering wheel with her left hand as she turned on the ignition with her right. There was only one thing she could do to try to make up for what she had—*hadn't*—done.

Abbie knew what Mrs. Merkel would want her to do. Abbie wouldn't just leave this attack up to the police to solve. She'd work as hard as she could to find the person who had done this to Mrs. Merkel and come up with enough proof for a conviction.

"I promise," Abbie said aloud, as if she were talking to Mrs. Merkel.

She pulled out behind the ambulance and followed it to Mercy Hospital.

CHAPTER THIRTEEN

A bbie arrived at the hospital just behind the ambulance and she followed the stretcher inside, telling the woman at the desk that she was with Mrs. Merkel.

The receptionist waved toward the nearly empty waiting room. "Have a seat," she said. "I'll let the doctor know you're here."

"May I borrow the phone for a second, please?" Abbie asked. "I want to call my mother."

"Here you go," the receptionist said as she slid a telephone across the counter. "Please be quick. Just punch nine before you make your call."

Abbie told her mother a brief version of the story, ignoring her mother's gasps and beginnings of questions. When Abbie had finished she asked, "Mom, could I stay until I find out if . . . uh . . . how bad off she is and how long she'll be here?"

"Of course," Mrs. Thompson said. "I can try to get Mrs. Erwin to come stay with Davy so I can be with you."

"No, Mom," Abbie said firmly. "It's okay. I'll be all right."

"Okay, honey. Call me if you need me," Mrs. Thompson said.

"Thanks, Mom. Bye."

Abbie heard the click, but as she was putting down the receiver she heard Davy say, "Wait, Abbie! Don't hang up!"

"Davy? Were you on the phone too?"

"Yeah. I listened in on the extension. I've got my notebook right here, so keep talking. What time did you get to Mrs. Merkel's house?"

"Time? Oh, about five-forty-five, I think."

"What time did the police and ambulance get there?"

"In about ten minutes. Maybe less. Listen, Davy, this isn't important. I've—"

"Yes, it is. We have to document everything. Do you have an alibi?"

"Do I have—" Abbie stopped in midsentence, aware that the receptionist was watching her with curiosity. "Davy, we'll talk when I get home."

"Okay," he answered. "But this time pay attention to whatever is going on. Think about who you saw at Mrs. Merkel's house. Remember

133

what the doctors say. And if Mrs. Merkel comes to and says anything—well, remember every word. Don't blow it this time, Abbie."

"I won't," Abbie said. "See you later." She hung up the receiver, giving an apologetic glance to the receptionist, and walked toward one of the rows of molded plastic chairs that lined the walls.

After what seemed like an endless wait, a voice spoke from beside her. "Ms. Thompson?"

Abbie turned to see a young man dressed in scrubs. "I'm Abbie Thompson," she said.

"I'm Dr. Phillips. They told me you're with Mrs. Edna Merkel?"

"Yes. She's a . . . a friend. Will she be all right?"

"We won't know that for a while. She was struck pretty hard on the back of her head with a heavy object. It fractured her skull. We've reduced the swelling and have stablized her condition for now."

"Could I see her? Talk to her?"

"You can see her, but Mrs. Merkel won't be able to communicate with you. She's in a coma."

"Will she be in a coma for long?"

"At the moment we have no way of knowing. She's in the intensive care unit, and you can visit her for a few minutes. If her condition improves or remains stable, we'll move her to a hospital room. Would you like to come with me?"

Abbie walked with Dr. Phillips through a pair of swinging doors into a white, brightly lit hallway. "What was she hit with?" she asked. She thought of the men Mrs. Merkel had threatened. "The police couldn't find a weapon. Could you tell what was used? Was it a tire iron? Or some kind of a tool?"

Shrugging, Dr. Phillips answered, "I don't know. There were two deep, pronglike puncture wounds. I have no idea what could have made them."

The doctor stopped at a desk, nodded to the nurse behind it, and held a door open for Abbie to walk through. "Talk softly in here," he said. "There are only a few patients in our ICU, but they need peace and quiet."

He stepped ahead of Abbie, leading her to the foot of a bed in which Mrs. Merkel lay, covered to her chin by a white sheet and a light blanket. Under the bandage that covered the top of her head, her face was pale, etched deeply with frown lines. Even unconscious, she looked dissatisfied and critical.

"Can she hear me?" Abbie whispered.

Dr. Phillips shrugged. "Maybe. I don't know."

Abbie walked to the side of the bed. Mrs. Merkel's hands were tucked under the blanket, so Abbie touched her shoulder lightly, patting it as if Mrs. Merkel were a small child. "It's me . . . Abbie," she said. "I'm here."

She waited for Mrs. Merkel to stir or to show some signal that she heard, but Mrs. Merkel gave no sign.

"Whoever did this is going to be caught," Abbie told her. "I'm going to find out who did it."

She waited, taking a deep breath as she tried to strengthen her resolve. "I promise," she whispered.

"Better go now," Dr. Phillips said. "You can come back tomorrow if you like."

Abbie gave one more glance at Mrs. Merkel. "I hope you heard me," she whispered, but there was no response.

As she followed Dr. Phillips from the intensive care unit, Abbie realized exactly what she had promised. Finding the person who committed this crime was up to the police, not to Abbie. What did *she* know about catching criminals? Shakily she drove home.

"Mom, I need to talk," she said when she walked through the door. As she and her mother settled down on the sofa in the den, she told her mother every detail of what had happened that evening.

From where Abbie sat, she could see her pajama-clad brother. In the dim light on the stairs, Davy crouched against the wall, knees drawn up. Hunching over his notebook, he was writing as fast as he could, probably trying to take down every word she was saying.

As Abbie finished her story and was answering her mother's questions, the doorbell rang.

Davy shot to his feet and scampered up the stairs into the darkness as Mrs. Thompson walked to the door.

Abbie joined her mother, recognizing the voice of the woman who was speaking. "Mom, this is Officer Amanda Martin," she said.

"Oh . . . please come in," Mrs. Thompson said, and Abbie was surprised to see that her mother was flustered.

"I have just a few questions to ask Abbie," Officer Martin said.

They sat in the den, and Abbie again watched Davy—notebook mashed against his chest—creep to a spot on the stairs where he could hear the conversation.

"I was told that you discovered Mrs. Merkel after the attack," Officer Martin said. "Will you tell me exactly where you were, how you made the discovery, and what happened?"

Abbie went through the story again. It was beginning to sound like the telling of a bad dream or a scary movie. It wasn't real. She'd wake up and the story would be gone. None of this could have happened. Abbie would go to Mrs. Merkel's house after school the next day, and Mrs. Merkel would complain, grumble, and tell Abbie to drive her to the coffee shop she was never supposed to set foot in again. Abbie put her hands to her forehead, pressing against a sudden pain.

"Honey, are you all right?" her mother asked.

"I'm sorry, Abbie," Officer Martin said. "I know this has been tough on you. But we need as much information as we can get as soon as possible. I hope you understand."

People were always asking her to understand, hoping she'd understand. Why should she understand any of the things that had been happening? Why shouldn't she just climb into bed, pull the covers over her head, and come out when it was all over?

"Yes, I understand," Abbie heard herself saying.

"You told Officer Bantry that you suspected that either the roofers or the man arrested for allegedly stealing cell phone numbers might have harmed Mrs. Merkel. Do you have a reason for these suspicions?"

"Only that all of them threatened Mrs. Merkel."

"Do you remember their exact words?"

Abbie squeezed her eyes shut, trying hard to remember. "When the police took away the roofers, the one named Mitchell said something like 'You're going to be sorry you did this.' Something like that."

"How about the other case—the one involving theft of cell phone numbers?"

"Well . . . he yelled some obscene threats about what he was going to do to her."

"Abbie, you didn't tell me any of this," Mrs. Thompson said.

"I'm sorry, Mom," Abbie answered. "I didn't want to worry you."

Mrs. Thompson sat upright, her fingers clenched together. Color rose in her cheeks as she said, "Just what is this Friend to Friend business all about? Are these girls being led into dangerous situations?"

"I don't work with the program, but I'm sure that's not the case, Mrs. Thompson," Officer Martin answered.

"Well, I'm going to find out from somebody who *does* know."

"Mom," Abbie said quickly. "It's not the fault of the Friend to Friend group. The elderly women who are assigned to the other girls in the program are nice people. They go shopping and to choir practice and have tea parties. Mrs. Merkel isn't nice. She tries to cause trouble for everybody. She thinks she's a private eye on a big case."

Mrs. Thompson sighed. "Since there's nothing you can do to help Mrs. Merkel now, I'll ask the Friend to Friend people to assign you to someone else. I'm going to make very, very sure you don't end up with another Mrs. Merkel."

Abbie didn't want to spend her free time visiting someone else, no matter how nice the woman might be. She needed all the time she could find to discover who had tried to kill Mrs. Merkel. "Please don't go to the Friend to Friend people, Mom," Abbie said. She didn't use Mrs. Wilhite's name and hoped that her mother had forgotten it. "I mean, I can help Mrs. Merkel by going to visit her in the hospital. I can talk to her. I can keep her company. Maybe I can help her recover and she can tell the police who attacked her."

"But these people you talked about—the roofers, somebody stealing cell phones—what if they come back?"

Officer Martin spoke up. "Frankly," she said, "we don't think any of those three individuals were actually involved in this crime. Con men aren't usually killers. They fleece their victims, then clear out."

"You're not even investigating them?"

"We're following through. There's an all points bulletin out for them, but I wouldn't be surprised if they haven't skipped bail long ago and left for other parts."

Abbie didn't agree. She wished Officer Martin could have seen the anger on Mitchell's face, the hatred on the face of the thief who spewed such ugly words.

Officer Martin added, "The crime against Mrs. Merkel is listed as a random attack during a possible robbery by person or persons unknown."

"Robbery?" Abbie asked.

"Yes. It's obvious that someone ransacked the downstairs. We don't know what was taken. I'd appreciate it if you'd come to the house with me right now and look it over. We need you to discover if anything is missing."

Mrs. Thompson objected. "Go with you right now? But it's late, and tomorrow is a school day."

"Mom," Abbie groaned, embarrassed. "It won't take long. I've only been in the living room and just walked through the dining room and kitchen. I don't even know if I'd recognize that anything was missing." An idea struck her and she asked, "What about Mrs. Merkel's nephew, Charlie? Shouldn't you get in touch with him?"

"We've been trying. We found his name and address on an insurance form on Mrs. Merkel's desk. Charlie lives near Dallas, so we've asked the Dallas police to try to find him."

"What do you mean, find him? What happened to him?"

"Nothing that we know of. We verified the address and phone number, but he doesn't answer his phone calls. He could be out of town or just at a movie. Until we reach him, you're the only one we know of who has been in Edna Merkel's house. Will you take a look and see if you notice anything missing?"

Abbie stood. "I'll be back soon, Mom," she said. "You go on to bed. I can let myself in when I get back." She could hear a rustling on the stairs. When she looked, she saw that Davy had left his hiding place.

"I'll wait up for you," Mrs. Thompson said firmly, but she looked at Officer Martin. "Just keep in mind that Abbie has to wake up early tomorrow morning to go to school."

"Yes, ma'am," Officer Martin said politely. She walked out to her car, and Abbie quickly followed.

Yellow crime scene tape was still attached to the trees and the porch railings of Mrs. Merkel's house.

Abbie stopped. "Do those mean we aren't supposed to go inside?"

"It's okay to cross the lines," Officer Martin

141

explained. "The detectives and the crime lab have finished their work, but no one's taken down the tapes yet." Leading the way, she entered the house.

The living room was colored a sickly yellow by the low-watt light that came from the lamps with tasseled, pleated shades. Trying to avoid looking at the bloodstained rug on which Mrs. Merkel had fallen, Abbie slowly walked around the room, trying not to step on books, papers, or knickknacks as she gazed at each object with full concentration. Something was missing. Something was not where it should be. But what was it?

With Officer Martin at her side, Abbie walked through the kitchen, then leaned against the counter, shaking her head.

"I only saw the kitchen briefly, as I was leaving the house earlier," she said. "The coffee cup is still where it had been. Mrs. Merkel was interrupted while she was drinking coffee, wasn't she?"

"Maybe," Officer Martin said. "It looks that way."

"The coffee cup's still here."

"The detectives would have seen it, and so would the crime lab."

"Didn't they take fingerprints from the coffee cup?"

"No. They'd only get Mrs. Merkel's prints. That wouldn't tell us anything."

"What if it was somebody else who drank the coffee?"

"That isn't likely."

Abbie sighed. She wished she had done what Davy had told her to do—pay attention. She'd been so full of herself and her own problems. Why hadn't she listened to Mrs. Merkel? Why hadn't she known it would be important to remember? "She said something about . . ."

"About what?"

Shrugging, Abbie said, "I don't know. Maybe it will come to me. Let's go back to the living room."

"What about the living room?"

"There's something about the living room that's wrong." Abbie walked through the kitchen door into the tiny dining room and on into the living room. She stood as still as she could, letting her eyes sweep around the room, checking every table top and nook. Finally, steeling herself, she glanced through the room, studying the carpeting, the sofa, the chairs, and the coffee table.

"Something is missing," she finally said. "But I don't know what it is."

Defensively she met Officer Martin's glance. "Look, I was in this room for only a short time. And most of that time I was sitting in a chair behind the open door, keeping an eye on the roofers, doing what Mrs. Merkel wanted me to do, so I really wasn't paying attention to the room."

Abbie sank into one of the upholstered chairs. She was so tired her body ached. Even her brain hurt. "Will you help me?" she asked Officer Martin.

"Help you? How?" The police officer took a step toward Abbie.

"Not that way. I don't mean I'm going to pass out or anything like that. Sit down . . . please. I need to tell you something."

Abbie told Officer Martin about throwing the rock through Jamie Lane's window and about the judge and what he had promised if she succeeded, and about Mrs. Wilhite. "I know she made it tough for me on purpose because I don't fit in with the rest of her model students," Abbie said. "She'll count this as all my fault and make it even harder on me. She may even refuse to assign another Friend to me. Please, if you write any reports that will reach the judge, will you recommend that I continue to visit Mrs. Merkel in the hospital? And could you tell him that you think it might help Mrs. Merkel come out of her coma and get better?"

Abbie bent over, resting her head in her hands. "I can't face getting thrown out of the Friend to Friend program like I was some kind of criminal no one cared about. And I can't even face another assignment."

For a long moment there was only silence. Then Officer Martin said, "Throwing a rock wasn't smart, but it doesn't make you a criminal, Abbie. And the idea behind Friend to Friend was to give elderly women the help they need, not punish a girl who is trying to make amends for what she did."

144

Abbie looked up. "If you knew Mrs. Wilhite—"

"I know Mrs. Wilhite." The officer paused, then said, "Your idea of visiting Mrs. Merkel and talking to her is a good one. One of those TV news feature shows did a whole program about how some doctors think that people in comas can probably hear what's going on around them. The hospitals play music to calm them—things like that."

"Then will you write this in whatever kind of report you have to fill out?"

Officer Martin smiled. "Better than that. I'll talk to the judge myself."

She held out a hand to Abbie and pulled her to her feet. "And you keep trying to remember what is missing from this room. If you do, give me a call." She handed Abbie her business card.

Tucking it into the pocket of her jeans, Abbie turned toward the front door. As she did she saw a man's face pressed against the window. With narrow, squinting eyes, he stared into the room.

Abbie screamed.

CHAPTER FOURTEEN

Officer Martin threw open the door, gun in hand.

"Hey! Don't shoot me!" a man yelled. "I'm looking for my aunt Edna. Edna Merkel."

Gun lowered, Officer Martin asked, "What's your name?"

"Charlie Merkel," the man said.

Her heart still loudly pounding, Abbie walked out to the front porch to join Officer Martin. Standing there, facing her, was a square-built man of over average height. His dark hair had thinned, leaving a bald dome that gleamed in the dim light from inside the house. He wore wire-rimmed glasses and a thin mustache and was probably somewhere between fifty-five and sixty,

Abbie guessed. His polo shirt was frayed, and on the area that stretched across his stomach Abbie could see what looked like food stains, even in the faint light. Mrs. Merkel had called him a bum, and the description seemed to fit.

"Step inside, please," Officer Martin told him.

She stood aside as Charlie entered the house, then followed him in, remaining between him and Abbie. "I'd like to see some ID," she said.

"Sure, sure," Charlie said. He tugged a wallet from his hip pocket and pulled out a driver's license. Glancing around, he remarked, "What a mess. Why is all that police tape outside? What happened here?"

"Did you drive to Buckler?"

He nodded. "I drove from Dallas. I just got here."

"Have you been in contact with anyone from the Dallas or Buckler police department during the past few hours?"

"No." He absentmindedly scratched at one arm. "I'm not in any trouble, am I? That parking ticket . . . I plan to pay it as soon as I get a few bucks ahead."

"Mr. Merkel, we've been trying to find you to inform you that your aunt was attacked by persons unknown at some time today. Are you telling me you're here just by coincidence?"

Charlie gasped and stepped backward. "My aunt's dead? Murdered? Oh, that can't be! I was just coming to see her."

"Edna Merkel is not dead. She has a fractured skull and is in a coma, but basically she's stabilized. She's in the intensive care unit of Mercy Hospital."

Finally Charlie was able to speak. "So she's not dead," he said.

"That's correct."

He suddenly seemed to notice the stains on the rug. "Did it happen here? Did somebody break into her house? Why?"

"At the present time, we think it was robbery."

"What did they take?"

"We don't know. Will you please take a careful look around the room to see if you notice anything that might be missing?"

Charlie turned awkwardly, and Abbie could hear the crunch of a glass figurine under his left heel. "She didn't have anything worth stealing in here," he said. "Just a lot of junk."

For the first time he took a good look at Abbie. "Who's this?"

"She's a friend of your aunt's—Abbie Thompson," Officer Martin said. "I brought Abbie over to check the house, to see if she could notice if something is missing."

Charlie studied Abbie with curiosity. "Do you know where she keeps her jewelry?"

"No," Abbie said. "I was only inside the house with her a few times."

"Well, I know," Charlie told Officer Martin. "I'll run upstairs and have a look."

"Lead the way," Officer Martin said. Abbie realized she wasn't going to let Charlie out of her sight.

Abbie followed them up the stairs. She felt too shaky to stay in that creepy living room with the bloodstains on the carpet.

There were two bedrooms and a bath upstairs. Charlie walked ahead of them into the bedroom at the back of the house and said, "This was . . . is . . . Aunt Edna's room. She kept her jewelry in a box . . ." His voice trailed off as he pointed toward the top of a high chest of drawers on which lay a small wooden jewelry box.

Abbie glanced around the room. Nothing seemed to be disturbed or out of place.

Charlie hurried to the chest and dumped out the contents of the box on the starched linen cloth that covered the top of the chest of drawers. Abbie couldn't see what had been inside the box, because Charlie was in the way, digging through the contents.

Officer Martin stepped up to join him, but he quickly turned and said, "Her rings are gone. One was a large pearl surrounded by diamonds, which Uncle Alf brought her from Hong Kong. The other he got in Australia. A gold dragon holding a big opal, with a small diamond at each side. Uncle Alf was in the merchant marine, but I guess you know that."

Officer Martin examined the rest of the jewelry. "This all seems to be costume jewelry," she said.

"That's right. Aunt Edna doesn't have much real jewelry. Just those two rings. She never wore them. They didn't do her or anybody else any good." He turned and leaned his back against the

149

chest of drawers. His lower lip slid into a pout as he shoved his hands into his pockets. "But what she did have is gone."

"Do you have any idea of the value of the rings?"

Charlie shrugged. "I can only guess—maybe ten thousand, twelve."

"Do you know if they were insured?"

"I know they weren't. Aunt Edna came to hate those rings because Uncle Alf gave them to her. After he left her she never wore the rings again."

Officer Martin made a note, then asked, "Do you know why she kept jewelry of that value in her house? Didn't she have a safe-deposit box at one of the local banks?"

"No," Charlie said. "As I remember, she asked about a safe-deposit box, but when she found she had to pay a yearly rental fee on the box she said it was a rip-off and she wasn't going to be suckered into it."

Officer Martin became businesslike again. "Will you please check her dresser drawers and closet to see if anything else might have been taken?" she asked.

Charlie bent to open drawers one at a time, then stood, shaking his head. "Nothing in them but clothes—blouses, underwear, stuff like that."

Abbie remembered that Mrs. Merkel had said she had two good places to spy from—the front window of the coffee shop and her back bedroom window. While Officer Martin's attention was on Charlie Merkel, Abbie walked to the back window, pulled the curtain aside, and looked out.

The window overlooked the backyards of two houses on the street behind Darnell Street: the house directly behind Mrs. Merkel's house, and the house just west of that one.

Abbie realized that a young family must live in the nearest house. Behind the wooden fence that divided the properties were a sandbox and a swing set. Toys were scattered throughout the yard. In the bright moonlight she could see that the house needed painting, and some of the shingles on the roof were so old they had cracked and curled.

The house next to it was very different. Although it was of the same vintage as the other houses in the neighborhood, it had been modernized in a number of ways. The entire back of the house had been enlarged and glassed in with wide sliding doors. There were no draperies to cut off the view, and lights were still on, so Abbie could see inside. Expensive lounge furniture in white wicker with puffy, colorful cushions and glass-topped tables decorated the room. The backyard, although smaller because of the expansion of the house, was beautifully lighted. Even in this late hour Abbie could see that the trim flower beds were part of a lovely, well-cared-for garden.

Which house had Mrs. Merkel been spying on?

The first house had no lights. The inhabitants were probably asleep. While the second house was well lit, there were no people about. Abbie let the curtain fall back into place. She had no idea what Mrs. Merkel might have been talking about.

Charlie strode to the closet and rummaged about on the shelves. Then he walked down the stairs—Officer Martin and Abbie with him—and examined the contents of the highboy in the dining room. Finally he stood in the middle of the living room. "Nothing else is missing," he said. "Just the rings."

"Thank you," Officer Martin said. She tucked her notebook away. "Now, if you don't mind, I'd like you to come with me to headquarters and sign a statement."

"You mean about the rings being gone?"

Abbie noticed that Charlie had begun to sweat and wondered why. It wasn't that warm.

"We'll also need to know what time you arrived in Buckler, and why you were here," Officer Martin said.

"I already told you—I came to visit Aunt Edna, and I just got into town. Came right to her house. That's when I looked in the window to see who was inside, and you scared the . . . you scared me by pulling that gun."

Officer Martin went on as if she hadn't been interrupted, "We'll also need an address in Buckler where you can be reached."

"I thought I'd stay right here. I've got a key," Charlie said. He glanced down at the stained carpet. "Only not tonight. Can I get the place cleaned up tomorrow?"

"I think so," Officer Martin said. "The crime lab is through, so there should be no problem.

While we're at the station I'll check with the primary detective on the case."

Charlie's nervousness seemed to grow. "Can this trip to the station wait?" he asked. "You've given me the bad news about my aunt. I'm concerned about her. I want to see her."

Officer Martin hesitated, then nodded agreement. "Just tell me where I can reach you."

As Charlie named an inexpensive motel down near the waterfront, a thought struck Abbie and she gasped.

"The coffee!" she said. "I remember! Mrs. Merkel told me she hates coffee. She never drinks it. She drinks tea."

Officer Martin stared at Abbie, her pen held in midair.

"The coffee cup in the kitchen," Abbie said. "It wasn't hers. Someone else drank half that cup of coffee. You need to take it in for fingerprints."

Abbie had watched Charlie Merkel carefully as she told the police officer about the coffee, but Charlie hadn't reacted. He calmly watched Officer Martin walk to the kitchen to get the cup, then looked at Abbie as if he were seeing her for the first time.

"Just who are you supposed to be? Nancy Drew?" he asked.

"Officer Martin told you. I'm a friend of your aunt's."

One corner of Charlie's mouth turned down wryly. "My aunt doesn't have any friends."

"I'm in a program in which high-school girls

are matched with elderly women. I drive your aunt wherever she wants to go."

Charlie didn't comment. He slowly and carefully removed a folded handkerchief from the pocket of his slacks and wiped it across his face, his forehead, and the back of his neck. "Where is that policewoman? When is she going to let me get out of here?" he muttered. He shoved his handkerchief back into his pocket, keeping his hand in the pocket too.

Just then Officer Martin walked back into the living room. She carried a plastic bag from Buckler's supermarket. Abbie could see the empty coffee cup inside. "Thanks for the tip," Martin said to Abbie.

"Is it okay if I go to visit my aunt at the hospital now?" Charlie asked the officer.

"Yes," she said. "Just come by police headquarters before nine A.M. Ask for either Detective Kraft or Detective Doheny. You know where the station house is?"

Charlie nodded. He even smiled at Officer Martin. And he had stopped sweating, Abbie noticed.

Officer Martin watched Charlie lock the front door and walk to his van. As he drove off, she said, "Come on, Abbie. This all took a little longer than I'd thought. Sorry. It's time to take you home."

"Will it be all right if I visit Mrs. Merkel tomorrow after school?" Abbie asked.

"Sure." Officer Martin smiled. "I'll make it all right."

When she arrived home, Abbie explained to her mother, "We're late because Mrs. Merkel's nephew showed up."

"Just hurry off to bed," Mrs. Thompson said, and gave Abbie a hug. "You need your sleep."

As soon as her mother had closed the door of her own bedroom, Abbie tiptoed to Davy's room. He was asleep, so Abbie showered and climbed into bed. She would have liked to talk to Davy about what had happened. She desperately wanted to talk to someone.

The coffee cup puzzled her. A person or persons unknown, as the police liked to say, had been in the house with Mrs. Merkel. Only Mrs. Merkel didn't have visitors. She didn't like them. She didn't want them. Her nephew, Charlie, apparently was the only person who was free to come into her house.

But Charlie hadn't drunk that coffee. He hadn't reacted when Abbie talked about fingerprints on the cup. He'd been nervous earlier when he thought he might have to go to the police station to be questioned and sign a statement. Why? Was it because . . . ?

Abbie sat up in bed, staring into the darkness. *Because he had the rings in his pocket,* she thought.

The jewelry hadn't been stolen earlier by whoever had attacked Mrs. Merkel. Charlie had fished the rings he'd described out of the costume

155

jewelry immediately after he'd entered Mrs. Merkel's bedroom. And he'd slid the rings into the pocket of his slacks.

Abbie remembered Mrs. Merkel telling her that Charlie needed a quick loan and she wouldn't give it to him. Was that why he took the rings? To get some quick cash? He'd said he didn't have enough money to pay a parking ticket. And he expected to stay with his aunt—maybe even hit her up for a loan again. Staying in a motel and eating out would cost him. It was easy to see why he'd want to sell the rings.

Everyone would think the rings had been taken by the attacker. No one would suspect Charlie. Should Abbie call Officer Martin and tell her what she thought?

She had no proof. She couldn't accuse Charlie on guesswork. Also, if Charlie actually had taken the rings, he would have hidden them somewhere by this time or found a buyer for them.

Abbie had to learn more about Charlie and about what Mrs. Merkel knew. She got out of bed, reached under the mattress, and pulled out the envelope Mrs. Merkel had given her. It didn't matter now that Mrs. Merkel had ordered her not to read the notebook. It might tell her what had happened.

As she turned the pages, Abbie saw that Mrs. Merkel's scrawl didn't make whole sentences. There were a few words here, a few there. They were hard to read, and they made no sense.

Maybe in the morning, when she wasn't so tired, the words in the notebook would be easier to understand. Abbie placed the notebook on her bedside table, then turned off the light. Sliding down in the bed, she turned on her side, pulling the blanket and sheet up to her chin. Maybe tomorrow everything would fall into place and she'd know what to do. She relaxed and soon slid into sleep.

In her dreams a dark shadow crawled onto her legs, holding them down. "You've got only fifteen minutes," a voice whispered in her ear.

Abbie struggled to get away. "Let me go!" she moaned.

"Abbie, be quiet!" Davy answered. "Mom's in the kitchen making breakfast, but if she hears you she'll come upstairs. We've only got fifteen minutes till she calls us. So start talking. I'll write it all down."

"Get off my legs," Abbie said. As Davy squirmed to one side of the bed, she sat up and told him about Charlie Merkel. "He took Mrs. Merkel's rings," she said, "but I can't prove it."

"Maybe you can when he sells them," Davy said. "If he took them to make money, he'll have to sell them."

"How would I know who he sells them to?"

"Crooks," Davy answered.

Abbie thought about it. "Maybe pawnshops. If he pawns the rings they'll be on display for sale."

"You could just tell the police," Davy suggested.

"I've got a better idea. I'll tell Mrs. Merkel."

Davy looked surprised. "She can't answer you. She's in a coma."

"But she might be able to hear." Abbie smiled. "Soft music and pleasant words aren't going to bring Mrs. Merkel around. But knowing her nephew stole her rings might. Mrs. Merkel's going to have to help me solve this case."

Davy looked at his watch, then at his notes. "We've got only two minutes before Mom calls us," he said. "Was there anything else?"

"Fingerprints on a coffee cup," Abbie said. She told him about it.

"Abbie! Davy!" Mrs. Thompson called from the foot of the stairs. "Breakfast is ready!"

Abbie flew into her clothes, shoved Mrs. Merkel's notebook into her backpack, and ran down the stairs. "Nobody else in the world has to wake up this early," she complained to her mother.

The telephone rang.

"Except Gigi," Mrs. Thompson said. "She called you twice last night."

Abbie answered the phone, but it wasn't Gigi. It was Gladys Partridge. "Dolores Garcia was the one who thought of getting your phone number from Officer Martin," Gladys said. "We're in such a muddle. We can't believe that it all happened. We're hoping you can tell us why."

"No one knows why Mrs. Merkel was attacked," Abbie said.

"Oh, we're aware of that. The officer I talked to didn't say why. It's the other part we don't understand."

"What other part?" Abbie asked.

"The part we want you to explain to us," Gladys said. "Granted, they had their differences, and no one could really blame him for being angry with her after what she did, and—"

Abbie interrupted. "Mrs. Partridge, wait a minute. I'm not following you. What are you telling me?"

"I thought you knew," she said. "His son said something about fingerprints on a coffee cup."

Abbie gripped the telephone. "Mrs. Partridge, please! What are you trying to tell me?"

For a few moments Abbie could hear two voices talking in low tones to each other. Then a stronger, deeper voice than Gladys's said, "Abbie, this is Dolores Garcia. A few minutes ago the police arrested Jose for attempted murder of Edna Merkel. Why was he arrested?"

CHAPTER FIFTEEN

As Abbie finished her conversation with Dolores, she realized that her mother and Davy were watching her intently. "The police arrested Jose Morales for the attempted murder of Mrs. Merkel," Abbie told them.

Mrs. Thompson sighed and leaned back in her chair. "Then it's solved. Thank goodness. Who is Jose Morales? Was he one of those roofers?"

"No," Abbie said. "He wasn't, Mom. He's an elderly man who was in Mrs. Merkel's book club."

Blinking with surprise, Mrs. Thompson asked, "Why did he try to kill her?"

"I don't think he did."

"Abbie, surely the police would know more about this than you."

Abbie didn't answer. She wasn't about to argue the point until she knew more about what had happened. "Mom," she said, "could I use the car today? Could I visit Mrs. Merkel after school?"

Mrs. Thompson nodded. "Yes, honey. Bette, in our office, offered to pick me up on days you need the car. I'll pay her back by giving her rides when she's in a bind."

"Thanks, Mom," Abbie said.

"Drop Davy off. You're both running late," Mrs. Thompson said. She stood and took her plate and coffee cup to the sink.

As Abbie followed with her own dirty dishes, Mrs. Thompson said, "Oh, by the way, your father called last night. He invited you and Davy to dinner tomorrow night." Abbie heard the hurt and scorn in her mother's voice as she added, "He wants you both to get to know Jamie."

"Tell him thanks but no thanks," Abbie said.

"He hopes to make it a special evening. He's made reservations at the Blue Water Beach Oriental Gardens restaurant for six o'clock."

How could he? Abbie thought angrily. That was their own special family place. "No way," she said. "I mean it."

Mrs. Thompson rested both hands on Abbie's shoulders, looking into her eyes. "Go with him," she said. "Please, Abbie. Politeness and civility are the only way to handle it."

"I don't like her."

"Do you think I do?"

Abbie sighed. "Mom, do you really want me to go out with Dad and that woman?"

"No, but I must say yes," Mrs. Thompson said. "As I keep reminding myself, there are some things we can't change, so we must accept them with grace."

Abbie shuddered. "What did Davy say? Does he want to go?"

"He's desperate to see his father."

"Okay," Abbie said. "I'll accept, but I won't like it."

Abbie was surprised when she was called to the office during third period and ushered into the principal's private meeting room.

As soon as the door closed behind her, a short man in a business suit stood from behind the table, reached out, and shook her hand. "I'm Donald Wright, an associate in the district attorney's office," he said. "I've been assigned to prosecute the Merkel case. I need to ask you a few questions."

Abbie sat down, but she didn't speak. She waited to hear what Mr. Wright would say.

"I was told you are a friend of Mrs. Merkel. Is that right?"

Abbie explained about the Friend to Friend program.

"Did you know Jose Morales?"

"I met him once at the book club meeting."

"Did you hear him threaten Mrs. Merkel?"

Abbie stiffened, clutching the arms of her leather chair. "I can't remember everything that was said," she finally answered.

"Just try to remember what Mr. Morales said to Mrs. Merkel."

"He . . . he was crabby with her, but she— you have to understand—she was mean and rude to everybody. She deliberately tried to get him into trouble."

Mr. Wright's eyes widened. Abbie could see she had said the wrong thing. She felt ill. This wasn't turning out right.

"Tell me how Mrs. Merkel tried to get Mr. Morales into trouble," Mr. Wright said, "and how you knew this."

Abbie knew she had to tell the truth. "Mrs. Merkel told me that twice she had informed INS agents that Jose and his son had hired illegal aliens to work on their yard crews. They had to pay fines. She said if it happened a third time, they'd be in terrible trouble. She seemed to enjoy having blown the whistle on them. She certainly enjoyed telling me about it."

Abbie leaned forward. "Mrs. Merkel got everybody in trouble; men who claimed to be roofers threatened her; a crook who was stealing numbers from cell phones threatened her. Why do you think Jose Morales is the one who attacked her?"

Mr. Wright leaned back in his chair, cleared his throat, and began. "As you probably learned

163

from the media, Jose Morales's fingerprints were on the coffee cup in the kitchen. He admitted being at Mrs. Merkel's house yesterday afternoon. He said he had come there to talk to her. She had called to tell him that one of his crews had worked in a yard on the street behind her house. There were three faces she didn't recognize, so she asked one of the men where his green card was. He dropped his clippers and ran, so she knew that some of the workers were illegals. She was going to inform the INS again."

"Did Jose say he hit her?"

"On the contrary. He insists he didn't."

"So maybe he didn't."

"He had motive. He seems to be the most logical suspect."

"What was he supposed to have hit her with?"

"The weapon of attack? Unfortunately, we don't know what it was. I was hoping you might have some idea about what it could be."

Shaking her head, Abbie said, "The doctor said it had two sharp prongs on it. It sounds like some kind of a tool—like roofers would use."

"Or gardeners."

"What about Charlie Merkel, Mrs. Merkel's nephew?" Abbie asked.

"What about him?"

"I think he stole Mrs. Merkel's rings."

"I don't have any information about stolen rings. You'll have to take that up with the police."

Abbie didn't give up. "If a thief stole Mrs. Merkel's rings, what would he do with them?"

"He'd probably sell them as quickly as possible for two reasons. One, he'd want to get them out of his possession before they were listed on the bulletin of stolen items that would be sent out to places like pawnshops. And two, he'd want the cash."

"If a pawnshop gets this bulletin and sees that they've got rings that look like the description of the stolen rings, would they tell the police?"

"They're supposed to."

"You mean some don't?"

Mr. Wright nodded. "There are always one or two. There's a pawnshop way down on Main the police always visit first." He tilted his chair back and suddenly asked, "Are you sure you can't tell me anything more about Jose Morales's threatening remarks to Mrs. Merkel?"

Startled by his abrupt question, Abbie said, "No, I can't."

"Maybe you'll remember better under oath." He pushed back his chair and stood up. "I'll call your parents and set a time and place for a deposition."

"I can't this week," Abbie said. "I mean, I've got to visit Mrs. Merkel in the hospital, and—"

"We're in no hurry," Mr. Wright said. "We won't go to trial until we've made our case, done our best to find the weapon, and lined up evidence from the crime lab and reliable witnesses."

"There weren't any witnesses," Abbie blurted out.

Mr. Wright leaned across the table toward her.

He stared directly into her eyes. "How do you know?" he asked.

Abbie stepped back. "I thought that's what the police said. May I go now?"

There was no point in going back to class, since the bell was going to ring in about ten minutes for lunch. Abbie went to her locker, took the green notebook from her backpack, and walked to the cafeteria.

Taking a seat in a corner that was farthest away from the cafeteria line, she opened the notebook and began to read.

It didn't take long to discover that most of what was written down had to do with somebody named I. C. As Abbie continued to read, comments like "expensive dress," "M'Lady Dress Shop, 3:30 P.M.," and "Bank, safe-deposit box" began to make sense. When she came to a notation, "Buck Steaver, not oil. Worked as mechanic, Beaumont Motors," with an address and phone number, all the scraps of information fell into place.

It was obvious that Mrs. Merkel was writing about Irene Conley. And now Abbie knew why Mrs. Merkel had suddenly told her it wouldn't be necessary to hack into Irene's bank records. She must have seen Irene go into the section where people could open their safe-deposit boxes. Cash could be hidden away in these boxes and not recorded. But why was Mrs. Merkel concerned about Irene Conley's money?

Buck Steaver, mechanic. That didn't sound like

a rich man who could leave a fortune to his daughter. What had Mrs. Merkel found out?

The bell rang, and Abbie put the notebook back inside her locker. During lunch period she listened to Gigi's chatter, and she smiled across the room at Nick. But her mind was on the notebook and its contents. Mrs. Merkel had bragged about being on a big case. Was this it? Did it have to do with Irene Conley and the bank president's murder?

After school Abbie drove to Mrs. Merkel's neighborhood. A carpet cleaning truck was in Mrs. Merkel's driveway, and through the open door she could see the crew inside at work. The roar of the motor carried down the street. Charlie was probably on hand too. Abbie was pretty sure he wouldn't allow the men to work in the house alone.

This would be a good time to visit Mrs. Merkel. She wouldn't have to worry about Charlie showing up and interrupting what she had to say.

But before Abbie drove to the hospital she circled the block, driving past the two houses Mrs. Merkel could see from her bedroom window. Young children chased each other across the front yard of the house that needed painting, while a young woman who was probably their mother shouted at them from the porch. Like a flock of birds, they suddenly made a sharp turn without slowing down, dashing up the porch steps and into the house. The door slammed.

Abbie stopped the car in front of the second

house, studying it with surprise. After seeing the modernization at the back of the house, she had expected similar changes at the front. The entire house was neatly maintained, red brick with cream-colored trim, but the exterior in front probably looked much as it had when the house was new. The old-fashioned porch, wide roof overhang, and small windows fit the modest neighborhood. Although the yard was tidy and well kept, it was nothing like the beautifully landscaped backyard, which was hidden by a high fence.

Neighbors could see only one face of the house. The expensive furniture, the gorgeous flower beds—these were a secret only the owner of the house would know . . . and Mrs. Merkel, who could see them from her rear bedroom window.

Abbie was about to drive on when a woman opened the front door and walked briskly toward her in a direct line. She was tall and blond and wore a knit suit that Abbie knew must be very expensive. Abbie remembered seeing her photograph and knew she must be Irene Conley.

"What do you think you're doing?" Irene demanded as Abbie rolled down the driver's window.

"I was just looking at your house," Abbie said.

Irene frowned. "I've seen you before. You were with that old bat Edna Merkel while she was spying on me, following me, writing down things about me."

"Uh, not exactly," Abbie answered. "I wasn't.

That is . . ." Taken by surprise, she couldn't think of what to say to explain Mrs. Merkel's behavior.

"Don't play dumb," the woman said. "The two of you even followed me into the bank."

"Not really. That is, I mean, Mrs. Merkel . . ."

Irene bent down, leaning against the car door for balance, and looked right into Abbie's eyes. "Don't make the mistake Mrs. Merkel did," she said. "If you're smart you'll stay out of other people's business. Somebody out there might decide to put a stop to your meddling."

CHAPTER SIXTEEN

Abbie left the neighborhood as quickly as she legally could. She turned on Main Street and drove south, toward the hospital.

When she saw Mrs. Merkel she'd tell her about reading her notebook and about Irene Conley's threat. Or maybe she'd explain about the notebook and not mention the threat. She wasn't really sure it was a threat.

Abbie groaned. She wanted to give Mrs. Merkel a reason for recovery. She wanted to tell her something that would jolt her out of her coma and make her recover enough to take a hand in the arrest.

I'll tell her about her rings, Abbie thought.

Charlie had said that his aunt hated the rings,

and Mrs. Merkel obviously couldn't stand Charlie, so the news wouldn't upset her. Instead, Abbie hoped it would make her wake up from her coma, wanting to solve the theft.

Abbie thought about what the assistant district attorney had said about a pawnshop on Main as she pulled up to a red light outside a shopping strip. A sign listing the shops on the strip was right on the corner. Among them was the EZ Loan Pawnshop.

Why not? she thought. She turned right and drove into the lot, parking nearly in front of the pawnshop.

The small window contained a jumble of interesting items—everything from watches to four Waterford goblets to a set of golf clubs. There were a few rings, but none of them looked like the rings Charlie had described.

Abbie had to press a button that buzzed back to let her know the door had been unlocked. She grabbed the knob and entered the store.

"Hi," she said to the owner, a small, shriveled man, who hunched on a stool behind the counter. "I'm looking for a ring."

He studied Abbie, then craned to look out the window at her car. "Go away, kid. I got nothing you could afford," he said.

Indignant, Abbie said, "I wasn't planning to buy a ring with my allowance. My parents will pay for it. It's . . . it's a birthday present. I want an opal ring . . . um . . . maybe an opal with a couple of diamonds . . . with an unusual setting. Have you got something like that?"

The man quickly threw a black velvet jeweler's cloth over the glass-topped counter. He reached inside the counter and pulled out a thin gold ring with a tiny blue stone. "I'll give you a good price on this," he said. "We give the best prices in town."

"That's not an opal," Abbie said.

"Even better—an aquamarine. Five hundred. I might take four-fifty."

"But I want an opal, with diamonds." Abbie looked the man squarely in the eye. "I doesn't matter how much it costs."

The aquamarine ring was whisked away, but the cloth remained.

"Haven't got one like that."

"Could I see what's in the counter under the cloth? Maybe I'll find something else that I'll like."

"No. Nothing here for you. G'wan home, kid. Your mother wants you."

Abbie left the store discouraged. Nobody was going to pay attention to a teenager. She wasn't even good at spying. Irene Conley had noticed her right away. How could she possibly hope to find out anything about Mrs. Merkel's attacker?

Idly, as she strolled to her car, she glanced into the window of the antiques shop next to the pawnshop. A Tiffany lamp first caught her eye, but under it stood something that immediately caught her attention—a traditional Asian bronze horse on a teak base, one front leg raised.

Abbie gasped. That was what had been missing from Mrs. Merkel's house! Her bronze horse! The thief must have taken it, too.

Abbie entered the antiques store and went straight to the tall, slender woman who smiled at her.

"At last, a customer," the woman said pleasantly. "This has been a slow day for business."

Abbie shrugged. "I'm really not a customer," she said. "I just want to ask you some questions about the horse you have in your window."

"Ask what you like," the woman said. She followed Abbie to the window. "Pick up the horse."

"I'm not going to buy it."

"That's all right. Pick it up."

Abbie reached for the horse, which—like Mrs. Merkel's horse—was a little over a foot long and a foot high, but she had to readjust her grip as she lifted it from the window. "Wow, it's heavy!" she said.

The woman smiled. "I wanted to give you an idea of how much bronze weighs, so you'd understand the cost." She named a figure, and Abbie whistled.

"A friend of mine has a horse like this," she said. "Except her horse has eyes of a shiny black stone."

"Probably onyx," the woman told her. "I understand that only a few of those horses were made. Those with onyx eyes are very rare . . . and valuable." She paused. "I'd like to see that horse. Maybe the owner could bring it in."

"I'll—I'll tell her," Abbie said.

As she placed the horse back on its stand in the window, Abbie shifted it in her hands and raised it, balancing the weight. For just an instant the horse's rear legs were up, pointing outward.

Two deep, pronglike puncture wounds. The realization that the heavy bronze horse could have been the weapon made Abbie start so violently, she almost dropped the horse.

Stumbling over her words, aware that the woman was watching her strangely, Abbie thanked her for her help and fled to her car. She had to get to the hospital quickly. She needed to talk to Mrs. Merkel.

"She's doing well, so she'll be moved to a private room in the morning," the desk nurse informed Abbie. "She's still in a coma, but talk to her pleasantly. Hearing friendly voices might just help her recovery. You can visit her for ten minutes."

Abbie nodded. She entered the intensive care unit and sat next to Mrs. Merkel's bed.

"It's me, Abbie," she said.

Mrs. Merkel, her face still pinched with unhappiness, lay motionless.

"I'm trying to do what you would do—find out who attacked you," Abbie said. "But I'm having trouble. They arrested Jose Morales, but I don't think he did it. I mean, even if his fingerprints were on your coffee cup . . . Well, that isn't

174

important to tell you. You'd know who you served coffee to."

Abbie reached under the light blanket and took hold of Mrs. Merkel's left hand. Mrs. Merkel's fingers were cool and quiet, lying still in Abbie's palm.

"You were hit from behind, so maybe you didn't see who hit you," Abbie said. "I think you were hit with your bronze horse. Did you know it's rare and worth a lot of money? Very few of the Asian horses have onyx eyes. That's what the woman in the antiques shop told me. She said she'd like to meet you. She wants to see your horse. I think she might like to buy it. If your husband gave it to you, you probably don't like it either. So you might be interested in selling it— if we can find it."

She paused. Her conversation wasn't going right. She'd try something else. "I went to the pawnshop looking for your rings. Charlie said someone stole them. Frankly, I think Charlie did. He didn't get to your house until after Officer Martin and I had looked around for anything that might be missing. I may be wrong, but I think Charlie took the rings while he went upstairs with Officer Martin and me. Charlie's big and broad and kind of hard to see around, so he blocked our view for a few minutes. But after all, how much time does it take to grab two small rings and slip them into your pockets?"

Barely—just barely—with the slightest of movements, Abbie felt Mrs. Merkel's fingers tighten around her own.

"I don't know how to be a private investigator," Abbie said. "I wish I knew what to do next. I think I'd better go over all our notes and take them to the police."

This time Mrs. Merkel's fingers quivered, then held fast.

"Please wake up, Mrs. Merkel," Abbie said. "I know I'm not doing a good job. When I stopped in front of Irene Conley's house to get a good look, she came out and told me to back off and stay out of her business. Was she in your house? Could she have been the one who hit you?"

A nurse walked up silently in her crepe-soled shoes and tapped Abbie on the shoulder. "Time to go," she said.

Abbie pried her hand away from Mrs. Merkel's, smoothed the sheet and blanket, and stood up. To the nurse she said, "She squeezed my hand. She knows what I told her."

The nurse smiled and answered, "That's nice, dear."

"Shouldn't you tell the doctor?"

"The doctor is fully aware of Mrs. Merkel's condition. Frequently friends or family members imagine that the patient is communicating, they're so eager for it to happen."

Abbie looked down at Mrs. Merkel. "Do you see what I'm going through?" she asked. "It's not only my dad who thinks I'm a nobody. If you want answers to who stole your things and who hit you, then you're going to have to wake up and help me."

176

Mrs. Merkel's nose twitched, and Abbie said to the nurse, "There! Did you see that?"

The nurse put a firm hand on Abbie's arm. "Come along, dear, and please be quiet. You don't want to disturb the other patients."

What do I do now? Abbie thought, and the answer came: *Talk to Davy.* Maybe if they put their notebooks together and compared what they'd found, they'd know what to do.

Davy was eager to help, and he was excited about seeing Mrs. Merkel's notebook. Their mother wasn't due home for at least an hour, so Abbie and Davy sat at the kitchen table, reading each other's notebooks. Finally Davy raised his head. "Irene Conley was stealing money from the bank where she worked. Maybe the bank president found out."

"I know," Abbie said. "The facts are in these notebooks. It's not hard to put them together. Irene had not inherited money from her parents. She got it from some other source and over a period of time. Was it the Gulf East Savings and Loan where she worked? Did Mr. Hastings discover Irene was embezzling?"

Abbie rested her head in her hands. "She might not be guilty only of embezzlement. She might have murdered Mr. Hastings. I think Irene was aware of Mrs. Merkel's suspicions. Mrs. Merkel liked to confront crooks with what she knew about them."

"We need another notebook," Davy said, "or at least a sheet of paper." As he tore a sheet from the back page of his own notebook, he accidentally ripped it at the top.

"Darn," he said, and jumped up to get a roll of clear tape from the kitchen drawer. He repaired the tear, picked up a pen, and said, "How do you spell *Jose?*"

"*J-O-S-E*. What are you doing?"

"Making a list of motives." He wrote for a few minutes, then said, "Okay. Listen up. Jose—to keep Mrs. Merkel from snitching to the INS. The roofers—to get even. The guy stealing cell phone numbers—to get rid of a witness. Irene—to stop Mrs. Merkel from telling what she had found out. Charlie—to get money from his aunt."

Davy put down his pen and looked at Abbie. "I've been thinking about Charlie stealing the rings," he said. "If he's so stupid that he'd describe the actual rings to the police and then try to sell them, he'd be just as stupid about trying to get rid of his aunt."

Abbie sat up and reached for the telephone. "I'm going to call Officer Martin. She might be able to give us some information about some of those suspects."

To Abbie's surprise, Officer Martin was in the station house and available. When Abbie explained what she wanted, Officer Martin put her on hold for a moment, then came back to the phone.

"Is she there?" Davy asked. He tore off a couple of strips of the clear sticky tape and played with them, twining them together.

"She's there. She's finding something." Something nudged Abbie's memory. "Davy, that clear tape—"

"Here's the information you requested," Martin said. "Mitchell and Eddie Krump left town and were last seen near San Antonio."

"*When* were they seen?

"On Wednesday. Matter of fact, because of a potential customer's complaint, they spent the night in the county jail."

"So they have an alibi. What about the other guy?

"Bud Kessler, who allegedly stole cell phone numbers. Bud was with his girl friend from Wednesday noon until past midnight."

"Would she lie for him?"

"Probably. But in this case they were with a group of people. Went to a rodeo and out dancing afterward."

"So Bud has an alibi too."

"Looks that way, but it doesn't matter. We have our perpetrator."

"I don't think Jose Morales did it."

"Can you give me a reason that would hold up in court?"

Abbie sighed. "No."

"I didn't think so. Can I help you with anything else?"

"I tried to find the stolen rings," Abbie told her. "I went to the EZ Loan Pawnshop on Main. The owner said he hadn't seen them."

Officer Martin laughed. "Right idea, wrong pawnshop. We recovered one of the rings. The shop owner had already sold the other, but we'll keep an eye out for it."

Abbie was curious. "If somebody bought the stolen ring, how will you ever get it back?"

"Sometimes the *Buckler Bee* lists stolen items. Occasionally a law-abiding citizen buys an object in good faith, discovers it was stolen property, and brings it in."

"And gets his money back?"

"Not too often, I'm afraid. The money is usually spent immediately by the person selling the stolen item. The pawnshop doesn't accept the responsibility, so the purchaser is out of luck."

Abbie told Officer Martin her theory, and Martin asked, "Do you think Charlie took the rings from under our noses?"

"He must have. Unless he lied to us about when he got to Buckler, he didn't show up until after the attack took place."

"It's possible that he did take the rings during his so-called search," Martin said. "The rings weren't pawned until the shop opened this morning."

"Could the owner identify Charlie?"

"As we expected, that pawnshop owner couldn't or wouldn't remember who had pawned the rings. His records listed what proved to be a fictitious name and address."

"One more thing," Abbie said. For just a moment she hesitated. "Remember I said that something was missing from the living room, but I couldn't remember what it was?"

"Yes."

"Well, it was an Asian bronze horse with onyx eyes. If you grabbed it at the head or in the middle, the heaviest part would be in the rear. The horse's back legs could have made the puncture wounds the doctor found."

There was silence for a moment; then Officer Martin said, "That's interesting, Abbie. We'll follow up on it, but promise me you won't try to follow Mrs. Merkel's bad example. You are not a trained investigator. You are not a member of the police force. Leave this case to us to solve, or you may find yourself involved in a highly dangerous situation. We can't always keep an eye on you."

Abbie couldn't make any promises. She tried to change the subject back to the weapon. "When you find the horse—"

"Chances are slim or none. Weapons have a way of getting lost. This one could have ended up in the gulf or could have been buried in a remote spot. It would be almost impossible to find."

"Who would throw it away? That horse is rare and valuable."

"Very few people would know that. They'd think of it only as incriminating evidence. Even though it was wiped clean, or even washed, enough traces of the victim's blood would remain for a lab to identify it. The D.A. likes to have the weapon on hand when he brings a case of murder, or attempted murder, to court, but even without the weapon, he has enough evidence against Jose Morales to prosecute him."

Officer Martin's voice became more abrupt and determined. "Abbie, I asked for your promise."

"I almost forgot to tell you what Mrs. Merkel found out about Irene Conley," Abbie said. "According to notes she made, Irene Conley's father, Buck Steaver, wasn't rich. Irene got her money by embezzling from the Gulf East Savings and Loan. She spent a lot of money on clothes, a car, and remodeling her house. What she didn't spend she put in a safe-deposit box in Unity National. Maybe Mr. Hastings found out. Maybe that's why he was killed. Maybe Irene did it."

There was silence for a moment. Finally Officer Martin said, "All I can say is that we are pursuing the bank investigation along a similar line. As for you—you can expect—"

Abbie interrupted. "Officer Martin, I know not to put myself in danger. Mrs. Merkel is the one who didn't know that. I'd just like an update, please. Did you find any evidence that Irene Conley was in Mrs. Merkel's house?"

"Abbie, I know you've put up with a lot from Mrs. Merkel. I can tell you this: We have an eye witness—a next-door neighbor—who told us that Irene Conley *had* visited Mrs. Merkel early that afternoon."

Abbie grew excited. "Did the doctors determine what time Mrs. Merkel was attacked? Could Irene have done it?"

"Don't get too involved with police work, dear. Don't learn from Mrs. Merkel."

"Please, just tell me something," Abbie begged.

"The witness saw Irene Conley leave the house. Mrs. Merkel stood at the doorway warning her not to come back. Now, as I was trying to tell you about your behavior—"

"Thanks, Officer Martin. I'll behave," Abbie said quickly. "Bye." She hung up the phone.

When she told Davy what the police officer had said, he shook his head. "We can't find that weapon any more than the police can. Whoever hit Mrs. Merkel could have thrown it off Longmont Pier into deep water. He could have driven it west on a farm road and buried it in rangeland where no one could ever come across it." Davy peeled the clear tape from his fingers and stuck the wad on the end of the table.

Abbie stood and reached for the tape, tearing off an eight-inch strip. "Watch," she said to Davy as she opened the kitchen door.

She held the latch in as she quickly slapped the tape across it, then shut the door.

"What did you do with the tape?" Davy asked.

"It's across the door latch. It keeps it from closing and locking."

"I can't see it."

"Neither could Mrs. Merkel when somebody used tape on her door to keep it from locking. I stepped on a wad of the tape. It was probably tossed aside after the attack."

"But you tried her door. You couldn't get in," Davy complained.

"That was after the tape was removed," Abbie said.

Davy looked at Abbie with admiration. "Cool," he said. "You're pretty good at figuring things out." He grinned. "Maybe you're learning how to be a good P.I. from Mrs. Merkel."

Abbie sighed. "It tells us *how*, but not *who* did it. And you're right about the weapon. If the police can't find it, then neither can we." She closed the notebook in front of her and said, "Sometimes I get scared."

"No, you don't," Davy told her. "I've been writing down all the things you've been doing. You're very brave, Abbie."

"It's not those things I'm scared about," Abbie said. "It's . . . well, I don't want to have dinner with Jamie Lane tomorrow night."

"Neither do I," Davy said, "but it's a chance to go out with Dad. We like the food at the restaurant and checking out the neat stuff around the fountain. We can pretend Jamie's not there."

"If we're rude to her, Dad will get mad at us," Abbie warned.

Davy thought a moment. "Okay. Then we'll be polite and say please and thank you and stuff like that. But we can still pretend she's not there and just talk to Dad."

Abbie began to laugh. She tried not to, but she couldn't help it. It was a strange kind of laughter because it gripped her like a vise and wouldn't let go. And while she was laughing tears rolled down her cheeks.

Davy stared at her in surprise. "What's the matter with you?" he asked.

Abbie wiped her eyes, reached for a tissue, and blew her nose. "To us, Jamie's nothing," she said. "For Dad now, you and I are nothing. Dad won't bother to notice—he's too caught up in himself." She laid her head down on her arms and began to cry.

CHAPTER SEVENTEEN

In the middle of the night Abbie awoke. She sat up in bed, shaking a little, as if she had broken away from a bad dream. Without even realizing it, Davy had given her the answer. It seemed clear now. She figured out where the weapon would be hidden from the police. She now knew who had put it there.

I should call Officer Martin, she thought. One foot was already out of bed and touching the floor when she doubted her own logic. She wasn't sure. She had no proof, and she had to be sure. She pulled her foot back under the covers, vaguely remembering when she was little and afraid of the monsters she thought hid under her bed.

Now that she was older, she knew that the

dark space under the bed was safe and empty, but monsters *did* exist.

Tomorrow is Friday, Abbie told herself as she lay back in bed. *Tomorrow I'll make sure the weapon is there.*

———————————————

At school Abbie saw Nick in the hallway a few steps ahead and trotted to catch up with him. "Hi," she said, warmed by his answering smile. "Will you be at Blue Water Beach tonight for your father's company picnic?"

His eyes lit up. "You mean you can go?"

"Not with you, I'm afraid. I do have family plans," Abbie said. "My father is taking my little brother and me to dinner at the Oriental Gardens restaurant there." She paused. "To get acquainted with his girlfriend."

"Oh," Nick said.

Abbie could tell he was trying to think of the right thing to say, so she quickly added, "We'll be there at six o'clock. Maybe we can at least see each other and talk a little."

Nick grinned. "You'll be there at six? Me too. There's going to be a mob, but don't worry. I'll find you."

"I hope we can have a real date if you still want to. You asked me to the prom. I should have given you an answer sooner. Thanks. I'd like to go with you."

"That's great!" Nick said.

He began to talk about a movie he thought

they could see. She tried to listen intently. Over his shoulder she could see Gigi grinning.

The bell rang, and Abbie went to class feeling good. She wasn't a nothing. She wasn't a nobody. She wasn't going to spend her life being afraid, in spite of what her father had done or might do in the future.

After school Abbie drove straight to the hospital. She was directed to the room where Mrs. Merkel lay hooked up to an array of IV drips and monitors.

"She has stirred, but she hasn't awakened," the nurse whispered. "Maybe if you gently chat with her it will help pull her back to reality."

Abbie waited until the nurse had left, then said, "Let's talk about what I've done while you've been asleep." She told Mrs. Merkel about reading her notebook and Davy's notebook, and what information she had given Officer Martin. "I know you didn't want the police to get all the credit for solving Mr. Hastings' murder and Irene's embezzlement, but somebody had to do something before it was too late, and as usual you are not cooperating. You won't wake up."

Now Mrs. Merkel stirred, making little grunting noises in her throat.

"I'm pretty sure I can find the weapon someone used on you. I think I know where it's hidden. I'll find out in a little while. The way I see it, nobody can prove what time your nephew Charlie arrived in Buckler, so about those rings—"

Mrs. Merkel's eyelids suddenly moved and

then opened wide. In a raspy voice she croaked, "You are a lamebrain! Don't blab everything you know where people can overhear you."

"I hadn't finished. That was just the beginning. There's a lot more," Abbie said. She stopped, her mouth open, suddenly aware that Mrs. Merkel was awake. She jabbed at the button to call the nurse. "You've come out of your coma!"

"That's obvious."

"Who hit you?" Abbie asked.

"How should I know? Whoever did it came at me from behind."

"Was anyone in the house with you?"

"If I'd seen someone, would I be lying here like this?"

"Irene Conley came to see you."

"With a lot of babble about how I could profit if I kept my mouth shut. Huh! I threw her out and slammed the door." Mrs. Merkel scowled at Abbie. "Now—about my notebook that you promised not to read—"

"I had to read it," Abbie said firmly. "You know that."

"I'm going to call Mrs. Wilhite. I don't need a snippy little troublemaker like you around."

Abbie took one of Mrs. Merkel's hands in her own. "Don't overreact," she said calmly. "You were assigned to me, and I'm going to be very hard to get rid of. We're going to find out who attacked you, and then I'm going to visit you and read to you and bring you something better to eat than hospital food."

"Are you just looking for trouble?"

"No," Abbie said. "I'm going to prove I can carry out an assignment."

Two nurses bustled into the room and one shooed Abbie out the door. "The doctor's on his way," she said. "You can sit in the waiting room if you want."

Abbie wasn't about to sit in a waiting room. She had to get home and get dressed for the worst possible evening in the world. And she had to make sure she could find the missing weapon.

At five-thirty Dr. Thompson picked up Abbie and Davy and took them out to his car, where Jamie was waiting. Jamie took one look at Mrs. Thompson standing in the doorway and didn't get out of the car. She merely swung around in her seat and smiled at Abbie and Davy, holding out her left hand for a backward handshake.

Abbie stared in amazement. The hand thrust at her, Jamie's hand, was sporting a ring. A gold dragon holding a large opal flanked by two small diamonds encircled her ring finger.

"This is Jamie," Dr. Thompson said as if purring. He turned the key in the ignition and drove away from the curb.

"Hello," Abbie said. She and Davy quickly glanced at each other before staring again at the ring. "Your ring is beautiful," Abbie added.

"Yeah, cool," Davy said.

"My darling Davis gave it to me," Jamie told

them, and then leaned over to kiss Dr. Thompson on his right ear. "I've got a friend in the business. He found it for us, and Davis insisted I just had to have it."

Abbie leaned back against the seat. She smiled to herself. The evening was turning out to be much more interesting than she'd thought it would be.

───────────────────

When they arrived at the Oriental Gardens, Dr. Thompson guided Jamie, working their way through a crowd of people to the dining room hostess. "Stay with us," Dr. Thompson ordered as Abbie and Davy turned toward the fountain. "There seems to be a much larger crowd than usual here, and we don't want to become separated."

"But Dad," Davy said, "we always look at the fountain first."

"Not tonight," Dr. Thompson answered. He said to the hostess, "I'm Dr. Davis Thompson. My party has a reservation for six o'clock."

"There'll be only a five-to-ten-minute wait," the hostess answered. She smiled as if pleased at their great good fortune.

Abbie glanced toward the main entrance. She caught only a quick glance of the back of a blond woman who had walked in but had turned and was struggling back through a group of people trying to enter the restaurant.

Abbie kept staring. The woman looked like

Irene Conley. Abbie moved her head to see better in the crowd.

The blond woman could have been anyone, Abbie admitted to herself, but she felt an even more urgent need to see if the bronze horse was hidden at the fountain.

"We've got five minutes, Dad," Abbie said. "Davy and I will be right back." She turned quickly before her father could answer.

They squirmed through the crowd in the lobby.

Abbie searched among the many fascinating pieces on display around the rim of the fountain. Where was the horse? She was sure it would be there, hidden among others like it, unnoticed even by the owners of the restaurant.

Suddenly she stopped, sucking in her breath. The horse was tucked in between four kimono-clad dolls, their paper umbrellas almost hiding it from view. She'd been right. The one person who knew the value of the horse had been unable to throw it away.

"Abbie," Dr. Thompson called, "our table is ready."

"Go ahead, Dad. I have to make a phone call," Abbie answered.

He frowned. "Not now. Don't be silly. This evening is just for the four of us. Stay here."

Abbie made her way to her father. "Dad." She tugged at his arm, pulling him with her. When they reached the fountain, she pointed at the place where she'd seen the horse with the onyx eyes. It was no longer there.

"Where is it?" she cried out, looking toward the doorway. Squeezing through the front door, shoving aside a group of people, was the blond woman.

Abbie saw enough to recognize her—Irene Conley.

As if pulled by a stare, Irene turned, giving Abbie a startled look. Then, ducking her head, she plowed through the crowd, bursting out into the parking lot.

Abbie struggled after her as she heard two voices. "Where are you going?" Dr. Thompson called.

And Davy yelled, "Wait for me, Abbie!"

Abbie ran as fast as she could, chasing Irene, who clutched the bronze horse as she dashed across the parking lot. Abbie's chest hurt as she tried to scream, "Stop!"

To Abbie's amazement, two uniformed police officers suddenly appeared and stopped Irene.

Panting and almost breathless, snatching gulps of air, Abbie managed to reach the police. "How did you know you should come?"

One of the officers calmly answered, "We've been keeping an eye on you, ma'am, at the request of Officer Martin."

"But how did she know I'd be here?"

"She didn't. We've been tailing you."

Abbie pointed at the bronze horse Irene was still holding. "Take good care of that horse," she told the officers. "Be careful about fingerprints. It's the weapon that was used when Irene tried to kill Mrs. Merkel."

193

"I didn't kill her," Irene insisted. "I've even got a witness that saw me on the porch with Mrs. Merkel, as I was leaving her home."

"I know," Abbie said, "but neither the neighbor nor Mrs. Merkel saw you slip clear tape over the door latch so it wouldn't lock and you could walk in later."

Irene shot a malicious glance at Abbie as the horse was taken from her and wrapped in a large piece of cloth from the trunk of the squad car. "You and that old hag just couldn't mind your own business, could you!" she growled.

"The police would have figured all of it out pretty soon—the embezzlement, the murder, and the attempted murder," Abbie said. "You gave yourself away, living with so many luxuries. Of all the suspects in the attack on Mrs. Merkel, you're the only one who knows about expensive objects. You're the only one who would know how valuable that horse is. Not Charlie, and not even Mrs. Merkel. I think you kept the horse and didn't throw it away because you planned to sell the piece. You're not only bad, you're greedy."

Abbie's father strode up beside her as Irene Conley was being put into a police car. "What's this all about?" he demanded. "What's going on with my daughter?"

The younger police officer said to Dr. Thompson, "I'll be glad to answer your questions, sir, but I think your daughter can do a better job of explaining to you what happened."

Jamie arrived, slightly breathless, balancing on her four-inch heels. She leaned against Dr.

Thompson, resting her left hand on his shoulder. Her opal and diamond ring flashed under the lights in the parking lot. Jamie looked at Abbie with alarm. "What terrible thing did Abbie do now?" she demanded.

"Why, she saved the day!" the officer answered. Then, staring at the ring, he added, "Ma'am, may I ask you about that ring you're wearing?"

"Isn't it gorgeous?" Jamie answered. She admired it as she wiggled her fingers.

The officer took some stapled sheets of paper from the squad car, read them by the beam of his flashlight, then turned to Jamie. "That ring fits the description of an item that was recently stolen," he said. "May I ask where you got it?"

"Stolen!" Dr. Thompson exclaimed.

"Stolen? It couldn't be!" Jamie screeched.

"What kind of a crook is your 'friend in the business'?" Dr. Thompson demanded.

"He's a very good friend. And he's not a crook!"

"I'm afraid that's stolen goods. I'll need you to come with us or give us some information.

Jamie tugged off the ring and began to shout at Dr. Thompson, whose scowl grew deeper by the minute.

Abbie walked away and leaned against the trunk of the nearest car.

Davy followed, leaning companionably next to her. "Bummer," he said.

"Poor Dad," Abbie murmured.

Davy looked at her with surprise. "I thought you were mad at Dad."

"I was. I am," Abbie answered. "But I I think I just stopped being angry and started to feel sorry for him."

Davy's eyes grew even wider. "You're sorry for Dad? Don't you mean you're sorry for Mom?"

"For both of them. I thought Dad didn't like us. I heard him say we were nobodies to him. I was wrong. I finally figured out that he doesn't like *himself*. He thinks of *himself* as a *nobody*. He's trying hard not to be himself, so he's got nothing and no one."

"Really?"

"Yes. I don't know why. I don't know what he expected to become someday or what goals he had for himself, but he thinks he's failed. Now look at his clothes, his car, his girlfriend. He's trying awfully hard to be somebody he definitely is not."

"But I love him. He's still my dad. You love him too . . . don't you?"

Abbie put an arm around her brother's shoulders. To her surprise, he didn't shrug it away. He moved even closer.

"In spite of everything, I guess so. I loved him better the way he used to be . . . but yes. I can't stop loving Dad," Abbie said.

"Hey, Abbie!" a voice called, and Abbie turned to see Nick striding toward her.

"Nick!" she called, realizing she'd almost forgotten about meeting him.

"I've been looking for you," Nick said. "I told

you I'd find you." He smiled. "Come on inside the restaurant. There's a ton of food on the buffet tables in the company's room."

"Food? Great," Davy said. "Can I come too?"

"Sure," Nick said with a grin, and Davy smiled back.

"We're going into the restaurant, Dad," Abbie called. "We'll be with the big party."

Nick took Abbie's hand as they walked away. "What's up?" he asked.

Abbie laughed. "It's a long story. When I've got time I'll fill you in."

"Tomorrow?"

"Sorry, not tomorrow," Abbie said. "Tomorrow I'm going to spend some time with my friend Edna Merkel, private investigator. She's solved a murder and ID'd the perp, and she needs my report to wrap up the case."

"Way cool," Davy said, his eyes shining.

Nick shook his head and then grinned. "About this story of yours," he said, "does it come with a translation?"

* * * * * * * * * * * * * * * *

Abbie didn't need a translation for Mrs. Merkel. As soon as she arrived in Mrs. Merkel's room, she pulled a chair next to the hospital bed and put down her tote bag. Before Mrs. Merkel had a chance to say a word, Abbie told her everything that had happened from beginning to end.

She'd expected Mrs. Merkel to be gratified, but Mrs. Merkel frowned. "*You* found the weapon used on me," she complained. "If I hadn't been stuck in this bed, I would have found it."

"But you have the evidence. Without that I wouldn't have had any idea it was the bronze horse."

The frown disappeared, and Mrs. Merkel looked puzzled. "What evidence?"

"The marks the horse's hooves made," Abbie said. "That's the most important evidence of all, and you're carrying it right under that bandage on your head."

For an instant Mrs. Merkel actually looked pleased with herself. Then she complained, "That's all well and good, but this evidence needs to be recorded. Have any of these nincompoops thought about that? Have the police taken photographs of the wounds? Have they measured the marks?"

Abbie reached into her tote bag and pulled out a Polaroid camera. "That's why I'm here. The doctor okayed photos, and he'll be on hand to measure the marks and rebandage the evidence. The police may or may not have taken photographs. I didn't ask, and it doesn't matter. We'll take our own. Good private investigators don't leave anything to chance."

Mrs. Merkel was silent for a moment. Then she let out a long, unhappy sigh. "Officer Martin was here," she said. "She told me I was officially retired from Buckler's Bloodhounds. She suggested that I learn to knit or embroider or paint with watercolors."

"I've got a better idea," Abbie said. She reached into her tote bag, pulled out a paperback book, and held it high so that Mrs. Merkel could see it. "This is a good, scary murder mystery," she said. "I'm going to read it to you. If you like it, I'll read more mysteries."

Abbie opened the book and began. " 'Herman knew someone was in the room with him. Though not a scrap of moonlight could ooze through the heavy curtains that covered the window, Herman blinked hard, desperately trying to see something . . . anything. In the silence he could hear ragged breathing . . . in and out . . . in and out . . . coming ever closer. Something soft and wet touched his bare neck, and Herman screamed.' "

"Huh," Mrs. Merkel scoffed.

As Abbie closed the book, placing it on her lap, Mrs. Merkel quickly said, "Don't stop. Since you haven't got anything else to read to me, you might as well keep reading that drivel."

"I thought you were going to tell me you can write better than that," Abbie said.

"It doesn't need to be said. I *can* write better than that—even on a bad day."

"That's what I thought," Abbie answered. She smiled. "So after we go through half a dozen mystery novels, I'll read the last book I bought. It's called *How to Write Mystery Novels*."

"Well, I suppose since you bought it, you might as well read it to me . . . not that I'll need it, you understand."

"I've got a laptop computer at home," Abbie said. "When you're ready, you can dictate. I'll write."

Mrs. Merkel sighed, this time with satisfaction, and relaxed against her pillows. "I guess I can manage to put up with you for a year," she said. "I just hope you're a better secretary than you are a driver."

She suddenly laughed, startling Abbie. "It just occurred to me. If I become a published mystery novelist, it will drive the book club members crazy."

Abbie laughed too. "And maybe Mrs. Wilhite," she added.

Mrs. Merkel waggled a finger at Abbie. "Quit wasting time, girl," she said. "Stick to what you came here to do. Start reading."

Abbie no longer minded being Mrs. Merkel's partner in crime. She opened the book and began reading. Her own tale was probably not as easy to wrap up as the mystery novel, but she now felt ready for any twist in the story.

ABOUT THE AUTHOR

JOAN LOWERY NIXON has been called the grande dame of young adult mysteries and is the author of more than a hundred books for young readers, including *Who Are You?*; *The Haunting*; *Murdered, My Sweet*; *Don't Scream*; *Spirit Seeker*; *Shadowmaker*; *Secret, Silent Screams*; *A Candidate for Murder*; *Whispers from the Dead*; and the middle-grade novel *Search for the Shadowman*. Joan Lowery Nixon was the 1997 president of the Mystery Writers of America and is the only four-time winner of the Edgar Allan Poe Best Juvenile Mystery Award. She received the award for *The Kidnapping of Christina Lattimore*, *The Séance*, *The Name of the Game Was Murder*, and *The Other Side of Dark*, which also won the California Young Reader Medal. Her historical fiction includes the award-winning series The Orphan Train Adventures.

Joan Lowery Nixon lives in Houston with her husband.